# CAUGHT IN BETWEEN

## LOVE IN A SUNBURNT LAND

## LEANNE LOVEGROVE

# ABOUT CAUGHT IN BETWEEN

*What do you do when the love of your life is marrying someone else?*

*Adele Bastian-Jones, wedding planner, has loved Luke since they were sixteen. After a whirlwind holiday romance, he announces he's getting married and begs Adele to plan the special day, in just one month! Planning the wedding of your intended betrothed is not what she had in mind. But she'll do it, and make it the best wedding ever, and in the process, get Luke to notice her instead.*

*Blake Kingsley, Luke's brother, was a legend of his sport until injury forced his retirement and the demise of her marriage. With declining health and sworn off women, he's living the quiet life on his estate in Bellethorpe, he tends to his vines and cares for his alpacas, and reluctantly agrees to host his brother's wedding.*

*Sparks ignite, crazy alpaca are on the loose, the weather is unseasonable, but still the wedding must proceed. Can Adele carry off her plan or will her head be turned in a different direction?*

**Fans will be delighted to return to the small town of Bellethorpe where they'll be reacquainted with old friends and meet new characters.**

*To the residents of small towns, thank you for the inspiration.*

# ANTHOLOGY - BUT NOT AS YOU KNOW IT

This novella is part of Love in a Sunburnt Land Vol 3 - but we've done it differently this year. Love in a Sunburnt Land Vol 1 was released in June 2021 and Vol 2 in June 2022.

They each comprised five novellas, by five Aussie authors - Rhonda Forrest, Louise Forster, Leanne Lovegrove, Susan Mackie and Emma Powell. Six months after the release of each one, we published the five stories as individual novellas.

The anthologies remain popular, but what we've learned in the last three years is that our readers *love a series*. So this year we're doing it differently. We're releasing the five novellas simultaneously, without first publishing them in an anthology volume. And each novella, while carrying the Love in a Sunburnt Land brand, is also part of a series for each author. While you'll find some common themes within these stories, each one is set in a different region or small town with their own vibrant characters and communities.

Caught in Between is the second in the Bellethorpe Series. I hope you love this story and will take a moment to explore the stories and backlists of my Sunburnt Land co-authors.

**Leanne Lovegrove**

# 1

————

Adele Bastian-Jones swallowed hard and bit back tears as the bride and groom exchanged their vows. It didn't matter how many weddings she planned in her job as a wedding co-ordinator, this moment got her every single time.

At this point, after delivering the bride to her soon-to-be-husband, she usually sighed with relief, then the emotion followed, quickly. Well, not always, some exchanges were perfunctory, others so over the top they were laughable, but the majority caught at the tenuous strings of her heart and made her weep.

This ceremony was one of those. The looks exchanged between the betrothed were dreamy and full of hope; each word spoken with love and affection. Adele searched for the tissues she always kept handy and dabbed gently at the corners of her eyes so as not to ruin her carefully applied make-up. More tears threatened as the groom lifted the lace heirloom veil over his wife's head and kissed her for the first time. Adele's lips parted, feeling the very essence of their connection and her heart swelled in her chest, caught up in the love affair playing out in front of her and the hundreds of guests.

The organ cued at the right moment and her pulse slowed. As rehearsed, the priest manoeuvred the couple to the signing table so they could formalise their marriage by executing the certificate.

Everything was proceeding as scheduled and on time. Perfect wedding planning.

Her mobile vibrated in her clutch purse and a bolt of frustration coursed through her. Everyone knew not to contact her while she was working. Being the wedding planner on the auspicious day that took many months, sometimes years in the making, meant she was on the clock the entire time until she collapsed into her bed that night, happy yet exhausted at the conclusion of another successful event and the start of another romantic journey. The phone kept buzzing and she pulled it out to check the culprit.

Luke.

Her body softened as her annoyance ebbed away like waves on a sandy beach heading back out to the depths of the ocean. Flicking her glance up, she caught the bride and groom smiling for the photographer in different poses: holding the pen to sign the certificate, heads bowed towards the desk where they sat, looking lovingly at each other. They'd be engaged for a few more minutes in attempts to capture this perfect moment.

Adele typed out a quick message to Luke that she was working and she'd ring him back ASAP.

As soon as the message whooshed away, her phone rang again. Bloody Luke; she hated breaking her own rules. He'd be the only person that dare interrupt her. But she couldn't be angry at him, she'd take his call anytime, anywhere. Realising he was on the other end of the phone, her body thrummed.

Peeking at the couple again, she raced behind a pillar to answer. 'Luke, hi! Can I ring you back?' She could barely keep the pleasure from her voice.

'What? You're home already? You aren't due to return from holidays until next week. Oh yeah, that sounded fabulous. I'd love to visit there...' Despite her request, he kept talking.

The deep and melodic tones of the organ echoed around the historic church. She'd been right, again; this tune was perfect. From behind the column, Adele watched the bride and groom stand and prepare to walk down the aisle for the first time as husband and wife.

She tuned back into Luke. 'I'm busy, yeah, right, news that can't wait. Okay.' Adele listened. 'No! What? Are you serious? Getting married. Wow.' Adele held her breath and feeling woozy reached out to prevent her fall. Her fingers slid around the smooth edge of the font while Luke babbled on. He had to be kidding, right?

Urgh! Adele ripped her hand off the fountain and scanned for the disgusting germs that must be crawling on the surface of her skin. Wiping her hand down her front, she then reached for the sanitiser in her purse. Holding the mobile between her shoulder and neck, she kept one eye peeled on the aisle of the church while she scrubbed her hands.

Her best friend, the one she'd loved since forever, was getting married. And not to her. 'But you've only just met...' she spluttered out the words. The bride and groom strolled past. Adele needed to get moving, get back on the job. Forcing one foot after the after, she turned towards the cloisters running along the outside edge of the church and leaned against the brick wall, the hard edges digging into her back.

Her mind processed fast. Luke had been away for a six-week backpacking trip around Asia. He'd met someone and now they were getting married. Getting married! She wanted to expel the words out of her mouth like an exorcism. Then she caught the end of the sentence as her best friend rattled on, excitement and joy in his voice.

'Me? You want me to plan your wedding? In a month's time?' There was no way she was planning Luke's wedding to a woman he'd recently met and fallen in love with. Especially when she wanted to be his bride. Her tummy didn't do a little flip-flop, it catapulted around like a washing machine on spin cycle.

'No, no, that's not possible. You can't plan a wedding in one month. There's too much to organise. It can't be done.'

Luke kept talking, providing reassurances. Adele interrupted. 'But what reception venue will we ever find on such short notice? Oh, okay. Your brother's Estate in a small country town. A unique Australian experience for your French bride.' The egg and lettuce sandwiches she'd gobbled down only an hour beforehand, threatened to race back up her throat.

With dawning clarity, Adele knew she would be organising Luke's wedding in some backwater called Bellethorpe, whether she wanted to or not.

## 2

_One month later_

_Sunday: seven days before the wedding_

Adele slowed her car as she approached the entrance to the Estate. She'd been driving for more than three hours; the local town of Bellethorpe a blur as she powered through to reach her destination.

The entrance was stylish with stone posts flanking a wrought iron two-wing gate in black steel decorated with intricate swirls. Over the top hung a superbly thick, heavy-looking length of timber announcing her arrival at _Kingsley Estate Vineyard_. Wow, impressive. This wasn't a two-bit show as her mum would say.

She may have underestimated this place.

On either side of the long drive were expansive fields of vines. Peering through the windscreen, she crept her Mazda 3 forward and followed the road. Up ahead was a Queenslander homestead with wide sprawling verandahs protected by a bull-nosed roof. White wrought iron balustrading bordered the house in the similar swirl to the gate with gardens of brightly coloured blooming flowers along its base. In contrast was a bright red tin roof. All shades of green bounced up at her from the grass, to the trees and shrubs. Adele's breath hitched. This place was beautiful. A perfect spot for a wedding. Any bride would be ecstatic to be married in this environment. Her heart sped up a little.

Reaching a circular drive, a white porcelain fountain sat in the turning circle with angelic faces spurting water. The water feature was surrounded by vibrant spring blooms at its base as part of a neat and trimmed garden. This place was too romantic!

To her left was a small car park where she found a spot and stalled the engine. Exiting the car, she performed a full body stretch, her limbs happy to be free. There were a few cars in the lot, but it was otherwise quiet. The tables and chairs along the decks were empty and no one wandered around the lawn. Odd for a Sunday afternoon. Perhaps everyone had already gone home after the weekend?

Adele twirled on the spot hearing a noise behind her. At the rear of the car park was a fenced paddock with lush grass from the heavy rain through winter. Now, in late September, the days were warm and the sun biting in the middle of the day. Not the premium time of year to get married in her opinion, but hey, everyone was different. At least it wasn't December.

Slamming the car door, she wandered towards the fence, straining to hear the sound again. She stood letting the serenity envelope her. It was all solitude, peace and quiet out here in the country. Closing her eyes, she soaked it up for the briefest moment, until, again, there it was... a warbling hum. A song? Music from a band? A bird? In the otherwise tranquil environment, the disturbance was out of place. Maybe that's where everyone was? Careful not to touch the timber barrier, she slipped through to investigate.

Peering around the corner of a nearby shed, the noise increased and her face lit up into a broad smile. Llamas! They were super cute with pointy ears and hair hanging into eyes in a small, triangular face. Luke didn't mention anything about pet llamas. There was an entire pen of the woolly creatures with coats of white, caramel, brown and black standing almost as tall as her.

A nudge to her back and she spun to face a rather large one. Why wasn't it penned behind her? Adele reared back. She wasn't scared of it, per se, she simply didn't want any part of it touching her. She took another step backward. It made that weird sound too; reminded her of the toy kazoo she had as a kid that she used to blow all the time to deliberately make her parents go insane. Now it sounded kind of cute. The beast kept making the sound without opening its mouth. Was it serenading her?

Didn't matter, she kept backstepping. It followed so close she could hear its intake of breath and feel the warm release. She repelled. Skipping in from out of nowhere, came another one. It was cuter, snowy white with a brown patch on its rear. Their coats were fluffy and she was sure it would feel nice to reach out and rub her hands through it, but she wouldn't. Imagine the dirt ensconced in that fleece? It would be revolting.

Adele's tummy turned over. Instinctively she shoved her hands in her jean's pockets. The animals paused with heads down, munching on the grass.

This was her chance. Adele strode towards the fence. The llamas were pretty and all, but she wanted distance between her and them. Almost safe and the big one charged in front barring her path. Shifting to the right, he shuffled too, back and forth they engaged in a dance where she wasn't quite sure of the moves. The smaller llama remained behind her a metre or so away, still eating happily. Her converse shoes sank into a moist patch of grass. Ick! She lifted her feet and jumped to the right. The animal matched her and bounced on its toes, its two pearly top white teeth on display. Each step she took, it followed. And that sound wasn't so cute anymore. Keeping her cool, she quickened her pace, the fence within reach. How could one llama be such a nuisance? In a lightning-fast decision, she bolted. The llama blocked her route. Adele's foot slipped and her body tumbled. Mud squished against her back and along her arms. Flinging her hands into the air, she flapped uselessly before holding her breath and connecting her palms with the cool earth. Slime slid through her fingers and she gagged. But then the animal pounced, its small feet resting on her legs, its face close, leaning in as if to lick her like a friendly dog, but instead it spat and warm liquid landed on her skin. Eyes closed, she screamed.

IN THE BACK FIELD BEHIND THE HOMESTEAD, BLAKE KINGSLEY inspected the leaves of his vines and cupped his precious

Verdelho grapes. They were his special batch; his favourite wine and they were in top condition for harvesting later in the year. Examining them made him forget about the dull throb of his temples; his earlier headache still lingering.

He was imagining the taste of the next vintage, rolling the tannins around on his tongue, when a scream pierced the air. He shot upright, listened and scanned the nearby fields.

Nothing. Blake didn't spot anything. Most of the lunchtime crowd had left. The cabin guests were either out visiting the sights or resting in their rooms...but something wasn't quite right.

With one last glance at his beloved vines, Blake raced between the rows and dashed across the fields. Reaching the cellar door, he spied something in the fenced area. Removing his hat, he shaded his eyes for a better look. Biscuit hovered over a person lying on the ground. Blake ran faster.

As he reached the paddock, Biscuit rushed over, graceful on his feet. Blake ran his hands up and down the animal's neck. Reassured, he wasn't hurt, he gave it a friendly pat and calm words and shooed Biscuit away. Coconut stood nearby munching grass.

Blake strode closer. It was a woman who wasn't moving. Shit, what if she was hurt and he was more worried about his pets? 'Are you okay?' He knelt beside her.

Her chest rose and deflated too fast, her breathing was loud and her eyes were wide. Blake whispered, 'It's okay. You're okay,' while he rubbed his hand along her arms and legs checking for injury.

'Stop touching me!' she screeched. 'You were just petting that grisly creature and now your dirty hands are on me!'

Okay, perhaps not seriously harmed. 'Sorry. Can you move?' He placed both hands on his thighs. The woman grimaced as she leaned on her elbows and manoeuvred to a sitting position. Her brow furrowed with the effort and her eyes turned into slits. Balanced, but still sitting on her bottom, she batted her hands around so that the bangles on her arm jingled.

'What is it?' he panicked.

She spoke through gritted teeth. 'I'm filthy!'

O-k-a-y. 'It's only mud.'

The woman groaned and examined her body. She wore sensible blue jeans, a coloured tee and white canvas shoes that were now brown. He offered to assist her up. She pulled a face but nonetheless slid her fingers into his.

Her hands were warm and soft, but slippery. Distracted by her touch, he pulled too hard and she collided with him, her full breasts brushing his chest. Quickly he embraced her to prevent her toppling backwards. Their mouths were only inches apart, her breath warm against his cheek while her eyes searched his.

This dishevelled, muddied woman was beautiful. But who was she and what was she doing in his field?

'Hi,' he said hoping his smile would break the tension. It worked and for a brief moment she smiled and her features lit up.

Until Biscuit returned and butted his nose between them. The woman jumped and swore but he grasped her tighter. Rejecting his grip, she pushed their bodies apart and his hand slipped from her back. He was now covered in mud, too.

'Biscuit won't hurt you.'

'Biscuit! You named your llama Biscuit? Is that because he eats people for afternoon tea?' Her tone was high pitched and

Biscuit's ears flicked.

Blake laughed but the animal was now more interested in him than her. Nonetheless he grasped the animal around the neck to lock him in place. 'Rookie mistake. He isn't a llama, he's an alpaca. They look similar.'

The woman moved two steps away and held her hands in front of her in a combative stance. 'I'm interested in the difference, really I am, but your alpaca spat at me and his saliva is all over my face and I would dearly love to wipe it off before I get rabies but my hands are caked in mud...so...'

Blood pumped through his veins but not from a potential deadly alpaca attack. He held his gaze steady on her ocean blue eyes surrounded by luscious blonde wavy locks tipped with pink. 'Trust me, he won't hurt you. He's only playing and interested in you given your crowding his territory. This is a fenced area after all.'

'He spat at me.'

'That's what they do. It doesn't mean anything. It's not an attack or to scare you, it's a reaction.' Regardless, the woman backed away. 'This is what we're going to do. You're going to walk over to the fence and climb through whilst I distract Biscuit and Coconut. I'll release them once you're on the other side.' With a nod of agreement, she walked backwards towards the fence until it hit her in the rear.

Blake led Biscuit to the food trough in the corner and petted him a few more times before exiting via the gate.

When he reached her, the woman was pacing, flicking bits of mud from her palms. 'Can you please show me the nearest tap?'

'Sure, follow me.' He strode a few metres across the yard and turned on a faucet where the water flowed fast. In silence, she washed her hands and the mud slid to the ground.

'You are filthy...' he said but she interrupted.

'Yeah, duh, Sherlock,' and she kept scrubbing as if she was trying to remove her skin.

'You're not going to like this but how about I wash you off with this?' She turned and Blake held up a garden hose.

The look was caustic. 'You're kidding right?'

'Nope. You're covered in mud from head to toe, and it's drying real fast. Before long it will set and be a pain in the arse to get off. Best get that grime off you now while it's soft. You can't even head inside like that, anyways.'

There was a pause where time stopped, she looked him up and down, and he imagined the cogs turning in her head.

'Sure. But I'm holding the hose.'

He shrugged and handed it over. Turning away from him, she firstly washed her shoes until they resembled off cream and then held the nozzle above her head like a make-shift shower. The water trickled down the bare skin of her arms and Blake swallowed, rooted to the spot.

'Your back.' His voice was throaty, like he had a bad hangover. 'There's mud across your shoulders and on your shirt and jeans. I can help.' He held out his hand and those eyes scanned him again. Nodding, she acquiesced. At first he kept the trickle light, but the grime didn't budge, so he upped the pressure until it was like he was bathing the alpacas after they'd rolled in the dirt and hay. He aimed for her pert buttocks looking very cute in her blue jeans. The water hit just the right spot.

'Hang on, time to move on...' she said.

Done, he turned the hose off and hung it in a perfect circle. Turning back, the woman faced him. Her wet tee-shirt clung to her breasts and his eyes couldn't focus anywhere else. His mouth was suddenly dry but he forced his gaze to lift. Her moist, pale pink lips were parted, her gaze intent. Her tousled hair curled into ringlets more than waves now. Swiftly her eyes diverted, to his chest, his legs and back up. She swallowed and cleared her throat.

'I need to get cleaned up.' Her voice was soft now, feminine and sweet.

Blake nodded, mute.

Blake swirled the yellow liquid in the long-stemmed glass. The restaurant buzzed with gentle conversation from guests enjoying Estate wines and canapes matched with a vista of the setting sun over the mountain ranges.

He had a million jobs to do, always did as owner and operator of the Estate, but he was glued to the spot. He'd shown the woman where to clean up and last he'd seen, she was wheeling a small case into the restaurant bathroom. He hadn't moved since. It was appropriate for him to check on her welfare, after all.

Sensing a presence, he looked up. His body twitched in the most inconvenient of places as she approached. The dusk light silhouetted her figure in the doorframe and provided her with an angelic glow. She'd changed into a short, colourful summer dress with spaghetti straps leaving her sun-kissed shoulders bare. Her long hair hung loose and framed her heart-shaped face. She glanced around the bar until her eyes landed on him and held them for a moment. He gestured her over and kept his eyes peeled on her every agile step until she arrived.

'You have pink hair.'

'And you say the most obvious of things.' But she accompanied the quip with a smile, her lips a shade lighter than her hair.

'I'm so sorry about before. I'm glad you're all cleaned up and not suffering any permanent injury.'

He was about to ask what she was doing in his alpaca den when she ignored his statement and extracted a disposable wipe and washed down the surface of the bar.

Instead he sought clarification. 'You're not hurt, are you?' and he reached for her hand. She pulled away out of his reach. 'I've washed my hands.' He joked.

'I'm sure you have,' she said with a smile but glanced downwards at his hands as if to double check. As if realising her gaze landed where it shouldn't, it shot back up and a slight flush entered her cheeks.

'I'm Blake. Can I buy you a drink to apologise for Biscuit's behaviour?'

'Adele,' she replied, appearing timid and small now in his presence.

'A drink?' he repeated.

'Oh, thank you, but that's not necessary...'

'Please, I insist. It's the least I can do.'

'Okay...'

Blake pointed across the restaurant. 'Take a seat and I'll join you in a sec.'

WHEN BLAKE ARRIVED AT THE TABLE WITH A BOTTLE OF WINE, SHE blurted out, 'I usually drink beer.'

He gave a similarly honest reply. 'Not here. This is a winery and it serves the best wine.' And that had been that.

First glass finished and she remained twitchy. It hadn't been an auspicious start to her arrival at the Estate and she was here to work, not meet the locals and have a nice time. Second and third glasses, or perhaps more, she'd lost count, and her anxieties had ebbed away.

Now they were two bottles down and too busy talking. Everything from her misadventure into his alpaca den, to stories of crazy brides. He'd topped her stories with tales of drunk cellar door customers and expert viticulturalists, but it was his impression of snobby sommeliers that had her in stitches. Her cheeks ached from laughing; there hadn't been a dull moment all evening.

She couldn't remember the last time she'd had so much fun. And, oh, how she missed it!

Blake was a conundrum. He was cuteness personified, funny and attentive, yet pure country goodness with polite manners, but was also damn hot, all rolled into one. For hours she'd longed to reach out and touch his stubbled and chiselled jaw. And he was so big! Or broad, really. When food arrived for them to nibble on (and absorb the alcohol, no doubt), she'd caught him glancing at the television in the corner where a football game was televised.

'Oh no, you're not a Collingwood fan, are you?'

He laughed, emphasising the creases around his eyes, and shook his head. 'No, hate them, but I follow the footy and the finals are only a couple of weeks away and if Collingwood loses today, they're out of contention.' Adele knew that. She followed the league too.

'I'm impressed. You're prepared to sit here with me rather than watch the big game.'

Blake didn't reply but gave her a scorching look that sent ripples straight to her core. 'Let me guess then. You look like a Bulldogs supporter.'

'You've got to be kidding me, right? No!'

'Okay, definitely, North Melbourne.'

'Closer.'

This banter continued until there were only two teams left. 'Well, we might be friends if you are a Hawthorn supporter, but if you barrack for Richmond, that's a deal breaker.'

It had been a joke. But his brow furrowed, and a deep frown appeared between his eyes. It disappeared in a flash as he recovered himself. Uncomfortable, he squirmed in his seat.

'Sorry, I'm joking. Football supporters are such a serious and competitive bunch, aren't we? I barrack for Hawthorn. It's a thick competition.'

'Well, let's hope it's not a Hawthorn verse Richmond grand final. That could be interesting.'

'Nah, we'd flog them.'

The tension eased in his hunched shoulders and a smile was back on his face. If only she could cool herself down. Where was that hose she used this afternoon?

'Do you play?' and her head tilted to the telly.

'I played a bit, back in the day.' He didn't elaborate and got lost deep in thought for a moment. Adele let the topic drop.

Made sense, though. He was fit-looking with a strong physique, muscles hidden under his plain blue tee-shirt and legs tucked snugly into his jeans. Heat crept up her neck at the recollection of his arms around her holding her safe from overbalancing and falling face first into the mud. He was strong and oh, boy, all man.

It wasn't only his drop-dead good looks that kept her enthralled, even though that helped. She wriggled in her seat too and pulled the top of her dress higher as it kept creeping low, revealing her bust. Occasionally she'd spot Blake with his eyes lowered and she swore his cheeks flushed.

Blake was good company: interesting and entertaining. She hadn't thought about Luke as often. She'd be lying if she didn't sometimes, well, perhaps, regularly, check her phone for messages. He was due to arrive in a few days and with the build-up to the wedding, they'd been chatting often. Something she loved.

So why was she enjoying Blake's company so much? It was shocking to her because Blake was very different to Luke. In size, demeanour, humour. Pretty much everything. And it had been a very long time since anyone other than Luke had caught her attention. And an even longer time since someone had looked at her like Blake did with his searing, intense gaze. An ache developed deep in her lower belly.

Outside the sun had disappeared hours ago, other patrons had drifted away, sated after a satisfying meal and wine. A couple lingered at the bar, sitting atop high stools. The inside lights were dimmed and the temperature had dipped, yet she was warm. It was the perfect summer setting with the open doors and easement windows allowing the gentle evening breeze to cool the room. Everything about the room exuded beauty. A perfect setting for a wedding. Except this wedding would be outside as per the bride's orders. But this room, with its antique furniture, ornate cornicing, chandelier lighting and vee-jay walls with a feature wall of stone, was historically charming. Paired with the mouth-watering food she'd tried, she'd be recommending this place to her clients if they were looking for a rustic, warm-hearted country wedding.

Blakes's leg brushed hers under the table and she came back to the present. She shivered and goosebumps scattered across her bare arms.

'Are you cold? I can fetch you a jumper?'

She ignored the comment and rose. 'It's time I bought you a drink.' She lost her balance and swayed to the left. He jumped up and steadied her, his grin pearly white. If the light wasn't so muted, she was sure those eyes would be sparkling. 'You're such a gentleman.'

Blake wrapped his arms around her. Adele leaned her body in, her head tucked into his chest, closed her eyes and inhaled his scent. It was familiar. From where? But then...she placed it. The same scent Luke wore. The walls closed in around her.

Blake?

This gorgeous man was Luke's elusive brother, the one he rarely talked about and she'd never met. Until now. And the owner of the Estate.

Her heart galloped and she felt his racing too, matching her pace. His head dipped and their mouths found each other. She should push him away, reject him, say there'd been a mistake. But his lips were soft, yet strong, like him. Tasted of delicious wine and sweet mint. His tongue dipped in and out of her mouth and her body came alive. Like an arid land deprived of rainfall, she soaked up the attention and craved more. A flick had been switched and now, she didn't want to turn it off. It was like they'd been building to this moment all afternoon. She wanted this sweet and funny man, now, here. This attentive man who'd cared for her, listened to her. Her lips pressed harder against his and somehow they fell back against the wall. He leaned in with pressure and their bodies aligned and felt each bump and groove of the other. Her body ached for his bare hands over her hot skin, his lips in places no one had touched for a long time. In their haste a glass knocked and fell to the ground.

'Follow me,' he said. And in that moment Adele was powerless to resist.

# 3

---

*Monday: six days before the wedding*

Blake's leg brushed against silky, smooth skin as he stretched out his long limbs. His eyes shot open and memories rushed in.

Last night. Adele in his bed. He rolled onto his side, facing her. Pretty pink strands of hair fanned across the pillow, one hand was tucked under her cheek while her face was angelic in slumber.

Who was she again? He'd never got around to asking and to be honest, as the night progressed, he hadn't cared. But now, the day after...

His gaze zeroed in on a freckle on the tip of her nose, but the intense focus caused his head to pound. Not even the sight of a gorgeous woman in his bed could ease the ache. And it wasn't from too much wine last night. He searched for paracetamol. Pills were stored in every nook and cranny in his place because he needed to treat his endless headaches. Bingo. A thin strip of capsules sat on the far bed side table. With one hand he reached over, gazing once more at Adele, the thin sheet outlining her contours. His body twitched at the knowledge of what lay underneath; his fingers keen to be trailing down the flawless skin of her back, moving around to the curve of her breasts.

He swiped the painkillers and rolled back. Facing away, he cracked the foil and swallowed the tablets. It'd take a few minutes to achieve even the slightest relief. The bed moved.

'Can't hold your alcohol, hey?'

Usually, he'd be annoyed at the assumption, but not today.

'Got some for me, too?'

The corners of his lips curled into a smile as he languorously rolled back towards her, holding out the packet and water. She leaned on one elbow, the cotton sheet revealing the tiniest view of cleavage. He became instantly aroused.

She took the pills. Her eyes darted to the water bottle, to his face, before she shook her head and placed the tablets away.

He traced his fingers along her arm, wanting to touch her once more.

'Last night was...amazing...' He plastered a smile to his face, but he'd lost his vocabulary. There was only so many ways to deliver words that should have been spoken before jumping into bed with a stranger. Blame the wine, again. 'I don't usually do that...'

Adele's eyes crinkled with amusement. 'You don't usually drink too much?'

'No, that's not what I meant...'

'You don't usually save damsels in distress from attacking

llamas?' She held up her hand, laughing. 'I know, I know, they're alpacas, attacking alpacas!'

Blake reached across and tickled her. The sheet released and he placed his mouth to her nipple. Adele threw her head back, her hand resting at the base of his neck. He moved to the other breast, licking, before advancing up to her luscious and inviting lips.

After a beat, she pulled away. 'You were saying?'

Those ocean-blue eyes sparkled at him, and he became mesmerised, trapped in their gaze. He needed to pull it together. Hard, well, when he was this close to a stunning, naked woman. And it had been a while.

'I don't usually pick up women I've just met and sleep with them. I need you to know that.' His words were strong, his demeanour intense. But it was important to him. Even at the risk of sounding lame because discomfort sat like a lump to his chest and he needed to explain. And to reassure himself that he was nothing like his father. Never would be. Or his ex-wife. Stupid really, because Adele didn't know either of those people or about his background. But still...

Her smiled dropped and she increased the distance between them by an inch. 'Me either. You were kind, welcoming and funny and plied with me with delicious wine until I couldn't resist your charm.' The intensity of her features relaxed once more.

'I don't regret it, not one bit. I simply need you to know it isn't my usual modus operandi.'

'Modus operandi. I like that. Applies to me too and I don't regret it either. But...'

He pressed his mouth against hers, preventing the words. His focus was on her for these precious few moments they had left. Her rosebud lips were parted and he tasted her once more and kissed her, softly, sensually. She paused their kiss, cupped his head with her hands, opened her mouth to speak...

A mobile phone rang. The sound was muffled and distant, but to him the real world crashed down upon them. Adele stiffened. 'That's me, let me check it. I am supposed to be working.' And he felt the absence of her embrace immediately as she rolled away and searched for her bag.

Working?

'Luke! Hello.' Adele shuffled fast, shifting to a sitting position on the side of the bed, covering herself. Facing her bare back he controlled his urge to lay a trail of feather kisses down her spine to the curve of her bottom. The skin of her torso was pale like porcelain.

Luke? Boyfriend?

'Yes, I'm here. This place is amazing, perfect spot for a wedding. Yep, I'll get on to that. Yep.'

A frisson of unease pulsed through him. Luke. Wedding. This was sounding all too familiar and his guts turned over. Pretending not to listen, he drained the remainder of the water and sat back. His head continued to pulse.

'Okay, brilliant, I'll see you in a few days.'

Ending the call, she fished around for something else in her bag as his mobile phone trilled. Adele pulled out a tube of sanitiser and rubbed a large drop into her hands. Then wiped the screen of the phone before applying it to the bedside table and placing her mobile face down.

Blake checked the screen of his phone. His brother. Reluctant to answer, he delayed but Adele was still fussing. 'Hey man, how's things?'

'The wedding planner? No, I haven't met her.' Blake leaned

against the bedhead and stretched out his long legs, no sheet covering his privacy. His brother prattled on, and he listened, watching Adele out of the corner of his eye. 'Sure, bro, see you soon.'

Simultaneously they turned towards each other, meeting in the middle of the bed. In synchronicity, they spoke.

'Blake, Luke's brother...'

'Adele, the wedding planner and my brother's best friend...' He laughed; Adele tittered.

'Honestly, I tried to say something this morning, but we were distracted and then the phone rang. And by the time I realised who you were last night, I really didn't want to stop.'

'No, I'm the stupid one. I should have connected the dots. And I should have asked more questions. But...' he shrugged. Did he care? Should he care?

Each digested the news. Luke had spoken of his friend and probably mentioned her name but Blake hadn't remembered. What would his brother think? Would he find out? Would he mind? He'd never expected Luke's best friend to be so attractive.

As it sank in, Blake laughed and cracked another smile.

But Adele hid her face. She jumped at his touch but didn't pull away, so he tugged her closer, until her body was tucked under his arm.

'Hey, it's okay. We haven't done anything wrong.'

Adele groaned. 'I'm so sorry.'

'What for?'

She looked at him then and her shoulders relaxed. 'It feels sorta wrong doesn't it?'

'Nope. You're not his girlfriend, that would be all shades of bad. You're his friend.' He didn't add that he would never, ever sleep with his brother's girlfriend. If given the choice, he probably wouldn't sleep with his friend either, but there was no moral code preventing it.

'Unless you're married or have a boyfriend?' He tried to keep his tone light, but the words were sour on his tongue.

'No, of course not! But, yep, you're right, we've done nothing wrong.' Even though she didn't seem convinced. The mood in the room electrified after it had been fun and playful before, and not forgetting, hot, after the intimate things they'd done together last night. It wasn't a night to forget. Rubbing his hands down her sides, he tickled her again, but it fell flat and Adele remained quiet.

Blake covered himself. 'Hey, look, a few minutes ago we agreed it was a great time and something we both don't normally do. Let's not get weird with each other and form regrets now. Okay?'

Her teeth nibbled at her bottom lip. If she continued to do that, he may not be responsible for his thoughts and roaming hands. But Adele nodded and offered him that dazzling smile again.

'I'm not looking for a relationship.' Her words hung in the air.

'Phew! Me either, I guess we're okay then.'

'Are you for real?' and she poked him with a finger.

Adele hadn't lied, he could tell. If he was wrong, he'd completely lost his ability to read people. 'To prove it, I'm going to make you coffee and breakfast. But my loser of a brother was light on with detail and I didn't realise you were arriving this early. I have no cabin available for you. They're all occupied till mid-week. You'll have to bunk in with me.' The idea both excited him and caused his eye to twitch. 'The shower is the first door on the right. Clean up and I'll show you to the spare room after we eat.'

It was a ball's up, or was it?

~

HOLY SHIT! THE EXTENT OF WHAT SHE'D DONE BORE DOWN UPON her like a heavy weight, crushing her chest. She was experiencing serious next day regret. Yes, she'd decided to sleep with Luke's brother and now she had to live with the consequences. Had she made a massive mistake? Had she ruined any slim chance she might have had to finally secure Luke's love?

Reality sank in.

Hang on, maybe Luke would be jealous? The thought dawned on her like a deliciously hot rising sun, warming her from the inside out. Would he finally realise what was right in front of him? That she was perfect for him? Yeah, right, Adele scoffed. She didn't know much about the relationship between the brothers, but she didn't want to make Luke jealous, she wanted him to love her. Her heart ached a little.

But why had she done it? What if she had ruined everything? She crossed her arms around her middle trying to supress the growing anxiety. Yes, she'd drunk too much. Yes, they'd laughed and she'd had a great time. But Adele knew the answer: it was Blake. The desire in his smouldering eyes had turned her insides to water; the way he'd looked at her had caused an ache to develop between her legs and she had throbbed with need. She was wanted, pure and simple and what a turn on it had been. Then his lovemaking had been gentle, oh, and the way he'd held her with such care and passion... Plus, he was bloody hot. They had good genes that

Kingsley family. And she was a single girl with no commitments, right?

Towel drying her hair, she entered Blake's cramped kitchen. She smelled coffee and Blake placed two plates of bacon and eggs and toast onto the small, circular table. The man could cook.

Had Luke ever cooked her breakfast? No, but he'd made many a dash to the early morning McDonalds drive-through after a bender the night before.

'I can find some accommodation in town for a few days. It's not that far to travel. I don't want to cramp your style and bunk in your personal space.' She sipped her espresso, impressed he had his own coffee machine.

Blake had placed a forkful of scrambled eggs in his mouth. 'We have heaps of cabin accommodation, but they're all booked until they are vacated for wedding guests. I'm sorry, you're here to work and there should be somewhere for you to stay. I feel bad. Luke stuffed up. But honestly, you're welcome. It's small but there's only me,' and he spread one arm wide indicating the space where they sat.

'Well, um, that's kind of you, and I really do need to be here, close by, obviously, to plan the wedding. Seems weird, though.'

'Really? I think we know each other well enough, don't you? It'll be cosy...and fun.'

He had that right. The bathroom was pokey, the shower recess so narrow her elbows had hit the glass shower screen as she'd washed her hair. The kitchen had only enough room for the tiny table. But like the homestead, these rooms had the authentic vee-jay walls with warm and inviting tones, plus it was clean. A single, tidy man. He impressed her.

'Can you show me where you usually hold your weddings?'

He arched an eyebrow. 'I'm not sure what Luke told you, but this is a vineyard. No weddings here, ever.'

'But Luke is getting married here this weekend.'

'Yeah, it's a favour, one I won't let him forget.' He drained the last of his coffee. 'I've got to get into it. Want to tag along? After I've tended to the attacking alpacas, I can give you a tour?'

'That would be great.'

Outside, Blake strode ahead, rubbing his temples.

In the light of the bright morning sun, Kingsley Estate was even more beautiful. The temperatures overnight must have dipped despite the time of year, and a light dew clung to the manicured grass surrounding the homestead. Taking a different route today, they entered the farm through the main entrance. A shop advertised ticket entry and depicted photographs of cute alpacas and packages available for purchase:

*Walk the alpaca*

*Feed an alpaca*

*Lunch with the alpacas*

*Paint & sip with an alpaca*

How strange; who knew you could do all those things with a spitting animal? Today they roamed the fenced areas behind the shop. A couple of early bird guests were in the front field crooning to a tall male they were trying to coax to walk with a rope lead. Giving up, they offered a spoonful of food mixture and it happily shifted from its spot. That same weird humming, thrumming sound permeated the air.

Adele rushed through the next gate at the same time as

Blake to avoid touching it. She caught his look; yes, she was odd, but clean.

'You want to wait here?' he gestured behind the secure fence housing the herd. Nodding, she agreed. The sun bit her forehead and she wished she'd brought her hat.

Inside the pen, the animals rushed at Blake and he petted each one and rubbed their lithe necks. Coming up behind him were a bunch of miniature alpacas. Babies!

Adele skipped through the fence without touching the timber planks and joined the throng. The animals raced around her as if in a game. The smaller versions were even cuter than their parents and not one of them spat at her. Blake distributed grains and hay. The adults gravitated towards the food; the babies happy to play.

'The crias like you.'

'The what?'

'Crias are baby alpaca.' he said. 'That one is Minty because he's all white, this here is Waffles, Sugarloaf, Nacho, Cherry and Tim tam.'

'I'm sensing a theme here. You like food?' she giggled and something popped inside of her making her feel alive. She didn't mind being around the playful animals as long as she didn't have to touch them.

'Suits them don't you think?'

One nudged her arm and she squealed, fisting her knuckle further into her pocket. Another baby bumped her butt and she curtailed it out of that area fast. Blake laughed at her departing back. Glancing behind, she watched him jostle with a particularly large male and engage in a game of what looked like tag. Her spirits lifted at the joy on his face; open, full, expressive. He loved these animals and they loved him. A dart of blue shot out from the left and into the melee of alpacas, a blue cattle dog joined in the fun. Then a Labrador. Blake threw sticks and balls and roused about.

Adele wandered away, heading towards the circular drive. She'd seen a rotunda yesterday and wanted to check it out. Ascending the three short steps, she stood under the roofed pavilion adjacent to the homestead on one side and row after row of vines on the other. She'd found it, the perfect venue for the ceremony. A tingle raced up her spine.

Standing tall with shoulders back, she stood at the centre of the platform. The world around her ebbed away, the edges blurring. Pachelbel Canon in D major played in her head as she imagined walking the red carpet towards the marquee, her heels not catching in the soft felt of the carpet, her betrothed standing to attention, waiting for her, smiling in her direction, her arm entwining with his, those she most loved in the world in the audience. A warm breeze tickling their skin as the sun cast a bright orange glow over those present as they professed their love for one another. Him leaning in to kiss her for the first time as his bride...

A dog barked and raced in amongst the vines and crashed Adele back to earth fast. Blake approached.

The problem with being a wedding planner is that she had played out her own wedding a million times in her head. Let's be honest, she'd been witness to exactly what worked and didn't, tried and tested successes and failure. And standing here, she was pretty certain, that few places were better than this.

'You're crazy not holding weddings here. You'd make a motza.' That wasn't half the sentiment she was experiencing but how to express it without sounding crazy?

He shook his head. 'It's not about profiting. We aren't a wedding venue. There's already plenty on offer. I'm really happy with our services and my focus is wine. The accommodation was a no brainer. A few hours from Brisbane and Toowoomba and people want a weekend away, to eat some great food, drink top-shelf wine and relax. Plus, we have plenty of land.'

'And where do the alpacas fit in?'

'I know it seems a bit strange...'

'Ya reckon?' she snickered. Her feet were firmly planted back in the here and now.

'When I bought the place a few years back, the owners were hobby farmers and kept a few alpacas with an assortment of other animals. They were selling to fulfil their dream of becoming grey nomads and the animals weren't an option to go with them. If I didn't care for them, they'd have been...disposed of, is a nice way of putting it.'

Adele shuddered. Blake continued. 'I wanted the vines and the restaurant and dreamed of manufacturing my own wines, but I knew nothing about animals. The cows and sheep dropped away,' Adele arched an eyebrow, 'died of old age but what started with a bunch of alpacas became more and the rest is history you could say.'

Another dog, a scraggy mustard-yellow chihuahua raced to his side and jumped up for attention. He petted it like they were best friends.

'So you're telling me that you couldn't get rid of the alpacas and now they've multiplied and on top of the winery, you're running an alpaca stud.'

'Sort of. They are pretty cute.'

'The babies are cute. The adults are spitting heathens!'

They both gazed out toward the horizon where there was nothing in their line of sight except rows of grapes.

'Honestly, though, this is the most glorious spot. You could hold ceremonies here in this gazebo, guests scattered around on the grass. The reception in the homestead with its old rustic charm and then the guests can tumble back to their cabins after too much of your great wine.'

Blake gazed at the vista and didn't reply.

'Juliette...' He looked at her confused. 'Luke's fiancé, Juliette, wants the wedding to be held in the great Australian outdoors. It's to be a unique experience. I'm picturing long rows of tables here and here,' she pointed, 'guests dining under the sparkling Australian country sky with our cool evening temperatures. There'll be a band playing in that corner and the dance floor, I don't know, here maybe in the rotunda, or perhaps a make-shift platform over there.'

When she turned expecting a response, his gaze landed on her and not the locations she pointed out. A sudden flush of heat warmed her neck at the scorching intensity of his look.

He shifted his feet and looked down...anywhere but at her. 'I've got to get back to work. Make yourself at home.'

Adele settled herself with her laptop and notebooks under the shade of a nearby large, old oak tree. If this was going to be the best wedding ever, she'd better get to work, too, and make sure everything was perfect.

# 4

---

*Tuesday: five days before the wedding*

The door creaked open as the hot water sluiced over him, easing out the worries of the day before it had even begun.

'Oh! I'm so sorry! I didn't realise you were in here.' Adele squealed and covered her eyes with both hands.

Blake wiped the shower screen clear of mist to see Adele. 'Want to join me?'

'What?' She peeked through her fingers before dropping her hands and running her tongue across her lips, her eyes everywhere but his face.

'I think you've seen it before...' He chuckled and turned sideways, buried his face in the stream of water and turned the temperature to cold.

Adele rummaged in her toiletry kit and ran the basin tap.

No point repeating his offer, she'd heard it the first time. He had been joking, but the urge to haul her into the shower with him, was strong. Somehow, he sensed Adele wouldn't have resisted, either.

Desire and discomfort fought for space in his mind and body.

Recovering under the blast of cold water, he asked, 'What's on the agenda today?' But he remained turned away, giving her privacy. Weird, but it seemed sort of normal to be talking to her while she brushed her teeth and he showered.

She spat into the sink before replying. 'I've got meetings in town. Confirming arrangements with the locals for Saturday.'

This surprised him. 'You've got locals helping with the wedding?'

'Yeah, sure. Do you know Caleb Stirling, the infamous chef who moved up here a few years ago from Sydney?' She didn't wait for a reply. 'He's agreed to cater the reception. Isn't that fantastic? He's doing what he's calling French-Australian cuisine.' Blake listened and let the water relax him. It worked after his sleepless night. Or perhaps that was the presence of Adele?

'Oh, and the lady from the flower shop is doing the bouquets and there's a band, but not from Bellethorpe, but out this way. Plus, the cake lady is local. Oh, but I can't remember her name.'

'That's great. The locals will be grateful for your support. It's been tough, you know with lockdowns and less tourist trade.'

'Of course, happy to help. Local is always best.' She seemed sincere. Adele paused, pouted into the mirror and applied lip gloss. 'What about you? You aren't making any money from the wedding?' Leaning back against the bathroom cabinet, she continued. 'It must be a loss to you for the accommodation and Saturday night trade in the restaurant. I hadn't thought of that before.'

And Luke doesn't care. But he didn't say that. 'No, it's all good, my wedding gift to the bride and groom.'

'Oh, okay. If that works for you.'

The skin on his hands was wrinkling and he turned off the faucet. Adele stopped talking as he reached for his towel and wrapped it around his lower half and slid the shower door open.

Her gaze slid to his torso and roamed there, lowering to the rim of the towel and back up in slow motion. An intense hunger stirred in him; a mixture of longing and attraction that was exhilarating and disturbing at the same time. He'd been honest about his intentions but hadn't banked on all these feelings...

He had to admit, he enjoyed having female company again. Not only in his bed, but someone to chat with over breakfast and in the evening. It had been so long since he'd had companionship that he'd forgotten how comforting it could be. That sense of not being alone. But company didn't equal a relationship. And no matter how much he liked having someone around, it didn't change anything. Having someone to talk to didn't mean you could trust them. Inevitably as time wore on, things changed, relationships transformed without you knowing it, interests developed elsewhere. He tried to avoid thinking of his ex-wife, but predicably, she popped into his memory, unwanted most times. Particularly if she featured in the weekend social pages with his old mates. His friends. Hard to ignore then. But that is exactly why he didn't buy the paper, rarely watched the news and only endured social media for business purposes.

Plus, little sleep last night meant his mind was open to an endless stream of thought. Dangerous. He needed to be busy even though the last thing he wanted to do was work. At least today, he wasn't rocked by a headache. Small mercies.

'Well, I'm off then, cheerio! See you later!' Adele waved and left, shutting the door behind her.

ADELE MISSED THE BUCKLE THREE TIMES AS SHE TRIED TO CLIP herself into the seatbelt before driving into town.

Fourth go she slammed it too hard, catching her fingernail. 'Ouch, damnit!' And she sucked on her thumb to numb away the pain. Her heart was beating way too fast and her concentration shot. Where was she going again?

Blake naked. It was all she could see. Yes, she'd tried to act cool and nonchalant, but, wow. His smooth broad chest without even the tiniest smattering of hair, bulging bicep muscles that curved into perfect mounds as he flexed his arms and his six-pack stomach. Putting the car into reverse she tried to ignore the aching twinge between her thighs. It meant nothing, right? Lust, that's all it was. She was entitled to be attracted to other people, particularly handsome men, and more so, those standing naked in front of her. It was normal.

Her focus was on making this wedding the best ever. And that meant ensuring everything ran to plan. The devil was in the detail. She exhaled a large breath and refocused.

Bellethorpe was less than ten minutes away. She passed *Finch Berry Farm* and *Appletree Orchard* and a castle! What the? She did a double take as she passed. Now her adrenalin was spiking for different reasons. Castle Belvedere looked genuine with turrets and fortresses and even a moat. A themed wedding venue? Something to store in her memory bank for later.

Next, she passed *Bellethorpe Christmas Tree Farm*. Oh! She released her foot from the accelerator, craning her neck to see fields of fir trees, shaped perfectly to pointy tips. The sign advertised a shoppe, café and farm with reindeer! Would she have time to stop on her way back and buy her mother a new Christmas decoration for their tree?

So many perfect wedding spots in one town!

These locations were on the outskirts of the district along with a few wineries. This Granite Belt region was renowned for its wine and short winter getaways. Entering the town, she crossed a narrow bridge over a wide fast, flowing stream and was in the main drag.

The day was back-to-back meetings so she could focus on the wedding guests arriving tomorrow. Appointment number one was the florist, followed by the caterer and the cake baker. But first coffee.

It was a congested but small centre with Main Street housing the important shops and businesses. Spotting a 'coffee' sign, Adele didn't hesitate and pulled into the nearest park. *Café Antiquities* appeared picture-perfect with a two-seater steel table out front surrounded by cute plants with red pots. The window displayed odd bric-a-brac with hanging clothes and a pine table with table decorations haphazardly piled on top. Inside was exposed timber beams with only a narrow passage to the rear where the coffee machine was grinding. On each side was a large accumulation of stuff – antique books if the colour of their tattered spines was any indication, paintings and clocks on the walls, old suitcases piled high, credenzas, comfy sofas randomly placed, and tables filled with an assortment of vases, miniature toys, teapots and crockery in mis-matched bundles.

The place buzzed with people and their chatter. An older couple stood behind the counter, the dockets lined up. The man serving wore an apron and held a pen in his hand ready to accept orders. He greeted her with a smile but before he spoke, the woman manning the machine stepped in. 'Hello, love. What can we get you?' She asked as she kept one eye on the dripping espresso and flicked a switch to warm the milk.

'Flat white on oat milk in a take-away cup please.' The woman repeated her order and the man wrote it down on his pad. She was sure their crockery was perfectly clean. Should she reassure them about this fact or make a quip at her own expense about her phobia? Too late, the moment passed.

'Thanks love, I'm Sheila and this is Peter. Have a browse or take a seat and we'll give you a holler when its ready.' She turned away with a smile and Adele noticed the man's left hand shaking. Sheila whispered into his ear and manned the coffee machine simultaneously.

Near the entrance, she'd spied a pair of antique lamps and she made a beeline back to them. The one thing she hadn't organised was a wedding gift. Not that she needed to, she guessed, as her wedding co-ordination services were without charge, and she had foregone any other income whilst planning Luke's wedding. Something they hadn't discussed but there's no way she'd charge Luke. A little niggle reminded her that Luke should have discussed this issue with her, but you know, they were friends. And she always looked after him. Plus, she was booked out for the next few months; things would be fine.

The lamps were an eye-catching emerald green glass framing a brass stand. In mint condition, she had to have them. Adele had no idea if Juliette appreciated antiques, or in fact, did Luke? Perhaps their tastes were more modern. Wouldn't matter. If their bedroom was chic, these would fit any style. The image of their shared bedroom caused a flash of nausea, so she brushed that thought away. Sheila called her name to collect her coffee and she returned to the counter.

'Oh, they are lovely,' Sheila said as she approached. 'A replica of an original pair made by Tiffany Studios that sold for $60,000 at Sotheby's. But I'll do you a deal,' and Sheila winked but Adele's stomach still swooped.

Sheila had enough energy for both her and Peter with her broad and ready smile with bright painted lips and blonde bouffant-esque hair. Peter now sat with his own coffee at a nearby-table. After coughing up the money for the lamps without blinking - anything for Luke - Adele put her coffee down in the spare seat next to Peter. There was a break in trade, but Adele had caught the flash of heartache flit across Sheila's face as she gazed at Peter, her hand to her chest.

'Thank you so much for the coffee,' Adele said by way of introduction, 'it's delicious and these lamps are the perfect gift for my...friend getting married.' Peter offered her a little smile in his well-creased face, his eyes distant. Adele discarded the plastic throw-away lid.

'A wedding, hey?' So, his hearing was fine. He continued, 'Sheila and I have been married forty years. Moved to the country years ago now and have run this place ever since.'

Adele started talking about the wedding and Kingsley

Estate, but Peter became confused about the location. Sheila stepped in and Adele had a feeling that occurred quite often.

'Remember the place out on Old Smith Road that Bob Hamilton used to run?' she explained to him, 'that's where the wedding is being held on Saturday.' Peter's head turned sideways in contemplation. 'Oh, yeah, he had those strange alpacas.'

Adele laughed. 'Yes. You're right and they're still there. They spit those things!' Sheila drifted back to serve other customers.

Peter told her they'd emigrated from England. Upon their arrival in Bellethorpe he became the local school bus driver before being a council Supervisor. But it was retirement and a shared love antiques that saw them now running the store. In between customers, Sheila whispered in his ear to clarify or insert detail into the stories he told. She also whispered, 'stroke,' and Adele understood.

'Peter,' she said and stood, 'thank you so much for the coffee and the chat but I must be off; I have a wedding to organise!' He offered her a lopsided grin as if he'd already forgotten who she was, and Adele's swallowed the lump in her throat.

Outside, she placed her purchases in the boot, slammed the lid shut and turned and ran straight into a mob of dogs taking up the entire footpath space. The leashes tangled around her legs as the dogs ducked and weaved.

'So sorry!' said the fellow apparently in control of the animals. He had his hands full and worked fast to untwist the knots. He commanded the dogs to sit and they obeyed and were rewarded with a treat. With the dogs calm now, the man worked the leads around one another until she was free.

'Thank you. You have a lot of dogs!'

'Oh no, they aren't mine.' He reached into his bumbag and

extracted a card. 'Lewis Ridgeway at your service from Perfect Pets of Bellethorpe. Very nice to meet you.' Lewis bowed at his waist in greeting and continued. 'We offer obedience training, kennels and boarding, dog walking and grooming. In fact any service required for your beloved pooch.'

Lewis addressed the dogs who were getting restless and petted them on their backs.

'Do you have a dog?'

'Um, no.'

A large golden retriever broke free from the pack, jumped up, its paws resting on Adele's chest, its mouth level with hers. Drool dripped from its jowls and she froze. Lewis intervened immediately, reprimanded the dog and took control once more.

Dog germs! They were the worst... but Lewis was completely oblivious to her discomfort.

'A shame. If you know any pet owners, please give them our details. Have a lovely day.'

Did she know anyone with dogs? Gosh, yes. Adele counted in her head. Blake must have five or six. But she didn't think he needed any dog help. A pity, Lewis was a nice, if not, a slightly unusual bloke.

Now truly late, Adele paused to furiously sanitise her hands first before striding the short distance to *Pretty Petals and Flowers and Gifts* for her meeting with the aptly named Lily. Her instructions were white blossom bouquets. Should be super easy.

An hour later, after designing the perfect posies of flowers with nothing too much trouble for Lily, Adele left the florist and made her way to Caleb's restaurant. Could that old catechism be true? People in the country were nicer than city folk? So far her research was an astounding yes.

Adele had read the scandal about Caleb poisoning celebrity singers at his restaurant in Sydney a few years back. Though he seemed to have bounced back, a knot of nerves formed in her tummy. She could never put the bride and groom, or the guests, at risk with less than perfect food. Always one to do her research, it had been a one-off incident that Caleb had paid dearly for with the loss of his restaurant and reputation. If the media was to be believed, the trade-off had been that he'd found love in Bellethorpe with a local country girl and together, they cared for his niece after the tragic loss of his sister. And his career had blossomed after he'd opened his local restaurant *L'Amour*.

Caleb pulled open the door before she had a chance to make her presence known. He was a tall fellow wearing dark jeans and shirt. 'Hello,' he bellowed and immediately kissed her on both cheeks. She recoiled and he noticed. 'You're new to town. You'll get used to it, everyone double cheek kisses here. It's the weird French thing going on. Sort of fun, though.'

Oh no! Something else for her to worry about...

As she recovered from the greeting (she put France on her list of places NEVER to go), she took stock of Caleb. Wearing a tee shirt, his tattooed right arm was on display, all black ink. She did an intake of breath. From behind her came a voice. 'I know he looks scary but he's as soft as melted butter.' Another woman, resplendent in a pink tee shirt emblazoning a large strawberry came forward and went to kiss her too, but Adele ducked and stood back. She was on to these townsfolk now.

To her credit the woman didn't flinch and smiled instead. She was the brightness to Caleb's dark.

'Oh, no, I wasn't...I'm from the city, we see all types.'

The woman flapped her hands in a gesture of never mind

and for her to come in. The restaurant was empty as it didn't open for lunch. Matching the desire in the name, the restaurant was decorated in warm tones of red and deep maroon and black trim. 'I'm Bridie. Caleb's partner. I'll leave you to it, honey,' she faced him. 'I have a crime thriller translation to finish before French class this afternoon.' She offered a good-bye of a long kiss on the lips. To her she said, 'you're in the best hands. Caleb will prepare the most delicious French feast your wedding guests have ever eaten.'

After she'd left, Adele asked, 'Is Bridie French?'

He laughed. 'Almost. She's fluent in the language, translates fiction novels in between running French classes at the school and helping her father run a strawberry farm. This town loves all things French.'

'Weird.'

'Yeah, you could say that but it's also distinct to this region and great for community spirit and by way of history, their descendants are French.'

'Oh, sorry. I didn't mean to speak out loud. I didn't know that, it's interesting.'

Her mind wandered. What a perfect place for Luke to settle with his French bride...

But Bridie wasn't wrong about the food. Caleb offered her a tasting selection of his ideas for each course. If there had ever been a doubt, it was washed away with each bite.

Adele knew restaurants were clean, they had to be. But she was very grateful to COVID for one thing: the better hygiene practices everyone now adhered to. Caleb wore rubber gloves as he served each dish and washed his hands in between; proffered fresh cutlery with each serve; used cloth napkins that were stiff with cleanliness and smelled of starch; and she'd seen staff spraying disinfectant on the tables as she entered.

It made her life much easier and avoided awkward situations that were once a common occurrence for her.

'I can't thank you enough. This is divine and the most wonderful blend of both French and Australian food. The harshest critics will be the bride and her family because they're French. You up for it?'

'Oh yeah. They'll love it,' he said all confidence and smiles. 'And anything for Blake.'

'Oh, but it's his brother, Luke getting married.'

Caleb understood. 'Yes, but if he's Blake's brother, he must be a top bloke.' Caleb continued. 'Blake is new to town, anyone who hasn't lived here for twenty years, is new, and he's one of the first to donate his time to a cause, or bottles of wine, usually. I used to love watching him play footy, too. Such a shame.'

Footy? Adele wanted to know more but Caleb's phone rang, and he waved goodbye.

She puzzled over the conversation as she offered her own cheerio. In her view, the two brothers couldn't be more different. Were they close? She guessed she'd find out soon enough. And what about footy? Like her, Luke was a mad keen Hawthorn supporter. Surely Blake hadn't played in the top league?

Who exactly was Blake Kingsley? And why wasn't he married with his own family? Luke was the same age as her, twenty-eight and Blake was the older brother, so perhaps in his thirties? He'd only owned the Estate for a few years; so what did he do before that? For the first time since they'd met, she pondered his quiet demeanour and calm outlook on life. He had a quiet intensity which she loved but what was really going on in that head? What would cause a young bloke to move to the country, buy a winery and hide away from the rest of the world?

Simone, the cake maker, was the granddaughter of Yvette who ran the French Kiss bakery. Everyone in town had connections, and if they didn't, they all knew each other and Adele sensed, looked out for one another. Simone had, like everyone else in the community been welcoming and kind and generous with their help. Likewise, as Blake had intuited, they were grateful to be involved, to get the business and offer their services. And compared to Brisbane, their prices were so reasonable! Incredible the difference a few hours from the big smoke could make.

Simone had nailed the brief. To be fair, Juliette had requested a cake that demonstrated Australia – think greenery, flowers, blossoming buds of eucalypts and Adele had sourced the piece de resistance and was happy to take the kudos. The only niggling worry had been how the baker would embrace the rather flamboyant idea. But Simone had been a star and accepted that the cake would be mounted on a rustic wooden log stand. The towering cake of four layers would be perfect. Simone needed immediate answers on the flavours of each layer and that lay with Adele to sort. Beside her on the front seat of the car were small boxes containing the options. Her task this afternoon was to try each one and choose. Sometimes her job could be very stressful...

Passing the Christmas Tree Farm, she fought her urge to stop; getting back with unmelted cake was priority. Instead, she kept her eyes peeled for the driveway entrance to the Estate and spotting it, indicated to turn.

Pulling in, she observed Blake kneeling near the grand pillars. Adele parked the car and got out.

'Oh gosh!' she exclaimed as she peered over his shoulder. Blake nursed what appeared to be a small dog with an enormous amount of white curly hair. 'What's happened?' She knelt beside him.

'I'm not sure. I don't think he's been hit. He doesn't seem hurt. Maybe abandoned? But he's shaking and scared.' Blake wrapped a towel tight around the animal. 'I'll get him up to the house and call for the vet.' Blake stood cuddling the bundle. 'Problem is the local vet services have been slashed and we share a regional vet, so unless he's close by, it might take a while.'

'No vet services, that's crazy,' Adele shook her head.

'Small towns and all that...' Blake let the words hang. 'Let's get up to the house. Can I catch a lift with you? I was in the vines when I heard him whining.'

'Of course, jump in.' She opened the passenger door. 'Oh, ah, just a sec.' and Adele placed the boxes on the rear seat.

Half an hour later, clean and fed, the dog was comfortable and sleeping. Adele brought out mugs of hot tea to the deck where Blake sat doting on the dog. She also bought the boxes of cake.

'What will you do?'

'With the dog? The vet will scan the microchip for an owner and locate them if he can. They'll be frantic, I bet. If the dog isn't chipped and not reported missing, I'll keep her.'

Adele sat next to him in a cane chair. The afternoon had lost its heat and a golden glow washed over the nearby valley. 'Wow, that's generous. You already have, what, four or five dogs?'

Adele thought of Lewis the dog trainer.

Blake shrugged. 'They were strays too and didn't have a home. Someone has to love them, and I can't bear them being destroyed.' He tickled the dog under the chin.

That left her lost for words.

'What's with the boxes? he gestured toward the collection on the table.

'Can you help me with something?'

He nodded.

'These are the options for the wedding cake tiers. It's going to be beautiful, but I must choose the flavours, today. So,' she opened one box, 'we have to taste test each of them.'

'You're asking me to eat cake and lots of it?' His grin was wide, but he kept petting the dog.

'Pretty much, yep.'

They worked their way through the slices. Adele tried each piece before Blake gobbled the remainder. 'These are so good.' He agreed.

'Is it a girl?' Adele nodded in the direction of the dog.

'Yep.'

She almost asked how he knew but swallowed those words back. 'A girl, so cute.' He looked at her funny.

'If we get to keep her, can we name her Marshmallow, you know, keeping with your food theme and because she's white?'

He gazed at her for a moment too long and her insides started to churn. 'You don't like it?'

'No, I love it. And you must choose this cake, what is it?'

Adele didn't want to release his gaze to check the tag on the box. But it was the rumble of a car on the drive that broke their connection. When Blake turned his head, a desolate emptiness overcame her. She wanted to reach out and touch him, feel the warmth of his smile again, the depth of his stare, his devoted attention.

The car arriving wasn't the vet, it was Luke.

'WELL, AIN'T THIS SWEET.' LUKE GULPED HIS PINT AND PLACED the glass back on the table with a thud.

Sweet wouldn't be the word she'd use, but Luke was being sarcastic. A whole range of emotions flooded through Adele. On one side of her, was the man of her dreams, the man she longed to notice her and love her in return. And on the other, a large gentle hulk of a man who had noticed her. And newsflash: neither man wanted a relationship with her. Plus, they were brothers. Flicking glances between the two she didn't know where to land her gaze, but in the end, as always, it was Luke who captured her attention.

The three of them sat at a square table in the restaurant of the Estate, low music rumbling in the background, a handful of guests enjoying the food and wine. The room was dimly lit, comfortable and warm. Adele fiddled with her cloth napkin.

'Nice place you got here, bro.' Luke slapped Blake on the back.

'What? You haven't been here before?' she quizzed.

'Never been any need.'

'How did you know it would be perfect for your wedding?'

Blake made a funny little cough and covered his mouth.

'Well, you've struck it lucky. This place is gorgeous. I've worked out where to hold the ceremony and the perfect spot for the reception, just as Juliette requested. The sun will be sinking behind the mountains, the lighting will be perfect and the setting romantic. Oh, and I was wondering...'

Luke cut her off. 'That's Juliette's brief. You can check with her tomorrow when she arrives.' Adele shifted in her seat. Blake's phone buzzed.

'It's the vet,' he said and rose to take the call.

Luke reached across the table, paused, but then patted her hand. 'It's so great to see you.' Adele lit up from the inside.

'So, you're in love!' Her voice was too high. 'How did this happen? How was your trip?' She had a million questions. Many of those involved how you fall in love with someone while on an extended holiday around Asia. And even if you did, why did you have to get engaged? Were the newly married couple going to live here or in France? That was one answer she didn't want. But most of all: did he miss her?

'I can't wait for you to meet Juliette, she's wonderful, Ad,' and he got a dreamy look in his eyes and directed his gaze to a faraway spot in the room. He'd used his pet name for her, but in the same sentence as expressing adoration for his fiancé. *Just how it should be.* But her stomach still felt like a lead ball had taken up position inside. 'Exotic, charming, stunning, long dark hair, elegant, slim, that accent...'

Okay, she got the picture. 'How did you meet?' At the question, his face lit up again.

'Funny story.' Oh yes, she bet. 'It was one of those crazy, cheesy situations where I reached for a drink at the bar thinking it was mine and she did the same, our hands connected around a cold pint of beer at a pub in Bali!'

Urgh, she forced her smile. That story made her feel immeasurably better. In her mind she'd imagined every scenario. Perhaps a romantic night on a boat cruise around majestic Halong Bay in Vietnam; or maybe at a temple where they had both taken quiet solitude in Bangkok or, Siam Reap where they'd stood in awe at the history and magnitude of the historic site.

'Incredible!'

'Sure was. And after that, we were inseparable.'

'And what does she do for work?' Adele squeaked out the words, frightened of the answer.

'She's a model. Has done shoots all around Europe. She's in high demand. Plus, she gets sent loads of free stuff and is an influencer as well.'

Adele sank back in her chair and luckily, Blake returned with Marshmallow cradled in his arms. The cute fluff-ball restored her spirits. 'What did the vet say?' Zac Coleman had turned up to examine the dog not long after Luke had arrived.

'No details on an owner yet. I confirmed I'll take care of her in the interim. Lucky she's not hurt and is in good health.'

'Aww, of course we'll look after her.' Blake placed the dog on her lap; Adele's hands shot into the air while Marshmallow balanced precariously before jumping to safety.

'Seriously, isn't there a pack of stray dogs running around this place already?' Luke's face screwed up in disgust.

'Luke!' Adele admonished.

Blake jumped in. 'There's plenty of room and I'm happy to do it.' It was a statement and the end of the conversation.

Luke stood. 'I'll get another round of drinks,' he said without asking what they wanted and moved away to the bar. Within seconds he was back, sloshing wine onto the table and announcing he was leaving. Adele recoiled at the wet and sticky surface. 'A guy at the bar is heading into town, I'm going to hitch a lift.'

'What? You've just arrived! We haven't even chatted yet...'
But Luke waved and moved away. Adele jostled around in her
bag for a wipe to clean the table. Finally glancing up, she
caught the flash of Luke's dark blue jacket as he dashed out the
entrance doors. Blake stared at her, his eyes squinting into
narrow slits, his expression one of scrutiny.

'Cup of tea in your room?' she suggested.

# 5

---

'Oh, thank God you're back! I can't find Luke. He's not answering his phone. Has he contacted you?'

Blake lifted the hem of his tee-shirt to wipe the sweat from his brow. He'd run hard this morning and was still catching his breath as he entered the kitchen.

Adele's mouth parted into a perfect 'o' and her eyes raked boldly across his bare stomach. He'd need to go for another run if she kept that up. Chugging down a glass of water, he flicked the kettle on.

Adele continued to stare, hand to one hip, a cup in the other, her cute eyes crinkled with concern while her pink hair framed her face. She still wore her pyjamas. Without answering he grasped her elbow and dragged her along to his bedroom.

'Well, I hardly think this is the time...' Her words spluttered to a stop as Blake swung the door open to reveal a body in slumber laying on his bed, taking up the entire surface. Luke. Snoring and fast asleep.

'What! How? When…'

Blake shut the door not caring about the loud bang and they returned to the kitchen.

'Luke crawled into my bed in the early hours of this morning. He's fine, I suspect. I'll sort him out, but you have bigger issues. Our guests have arrived.'

Adele didn't reply, lost in some sort of la la land. 'Adele. Juliette and her family have arrived.' Her eyes went saucer wide then.

'Right about now, they'll be unloading their luggage.'

'Argh!' she screeched and skidded out of the kitchen in her bare feet, running outside. The door slammed shut. Forgetting his tea, he quickly drank another glass of water to wash down his Panadol and followed.

When he reached her side, the French family were circling her, talking amongst themselves. They parted as a tall woman with luscious dark locks came forward. She nursed an oversized handbag and was meticulously turned out in light-coloured trousers and what appeared to be a silk cream top. Her stiletto heels clacked on the concrete drive. Her smile flashed, steely and fierce.

'Dog sleepwear matching your strands of pink hair?' Her voice incredulous and her accent thick. Blake had to admit, it ran like honey over his skin.

To her credit, Adele didn't blink. 'They are Peter Alexander and I love daschunds. Doesn't everybody?' She did not defend her hair.

By way of reply, Adele received a once over from the woman that was nothing like the hot glance she'd poured over him only moments before. This one was filled with scorn. Blake took a large intake of breath.

Adele laughed falsely, spotted him and jumped into action. 'Yes, well, it's lovely to meet you. I'm Adele, Luke's best friend and your wedding planner. It's been such a pleasure organising everything for your special day. This is Blake,' and she stood next to him, their bodies almost touching, presenting as a united force.

'Hello,' he said, extended his hand in greeting and then lost his words. He wracked his brain for her name but could not remember. 'Hello,' he repeated buying time. Moisture formed on his brow, this time not from his strenuous run. Shit. The problem with his short-term memory caught him at the most inconvenient of times.

'Juliette,' Adele jumped in, casting him a quizzical look. 'Juliette, this is Blake, Luke's brother.'

Juliette shook his hand with more interest than she'd shown in Adele. 'Thank you so much for allowing us to use your beautiful vineyard,' she said taking in her surroundings. Was she purring? 'Luke and I are very grateful. And my family, too. They are learning about the Australian countryside.' She slapped a bug on her arm. 'And the insects, too.'

'You're welcome, Juliette. Let me show your family to their accommodation.'

'But where is Luke? He arrived yesterday, yes?' Juliette scanned the area.

The extended family moved away with their suitcases and Adele stepped backwards to let them pass. Marshmallow bounced over and ran in between her legs. Adele shrieked, fell backwards and hit the hard edge of the fountain in the middle of the drive. The dog leapt on top of her and she threw her head around to avoid its licks.

'Are you okay?' Blake asked and retrieved the dog from her chest.

Shuffling forward she balanced herself and lifted her hands. They were covered in mulch from the garden bed. 'Argh!' and she flapped her hands around flinging mud bits.

'Adele,' he whispered close to her ear and lifted her under the arms. 'It's just dirt.' Standing together, he used his shirt to brush away the errant clumps. As the sludge fell to the ground, she dry-retched.

'You're here!' A voice yelled from the verandah of the house. Hero and saviour of the day, Luke bounded down the small flight of stairs over to his girlfriend and family, fully awake, dressed and smiling.

THE DAY HAD WARMED CONSIDERABLY SO ADELE SWUNG OPEN THE casement windows to allow the afternoon breeze to drift in. Turning back to the cellar door room, she smiled. It was inviting and beautiful with the fresh flowers and greenery she'd sourced from Lily and the tea candles glowing in the gentle afternoon light.

A perfect setting if she said so herself, and she did.

But neither Blake nor the family had arrived yet. Nerves knotted in her tummy.

Juliette's family had the morning at leisure: to explore the grounds, enjoy a late brunch or read and relax. However, this afternoon, she'd organised a special treat: a Kingsley Estate wine tasting. You can't visit an Australian winery and not taste the wines, she figured. And the French loved *le vin*. Checking the time again, she scanned the room and peered down the path leading to the building.

Someone entered from the rear. 'Hello there!'

Heavy boots stomped across the polished concrete floor. The shoes belonged to a tall man wearing a bright red checked flannelette with work jeans. His beard was grey and long, his eyes and mouth lined with age. He stretched out his arm on approach. 'I'm Cam, you must be Adele.'

She returned the pressure of his firm handshake. 'Sure am. Nice to meet you Cam. How can I help you?'

'Well, as it turns out, I'm helping you. Young lad, Blake, he's a bit under the weather and is resting so he asked me to do the wine tasting.'

'Oh.' Adele pressed her lips tight. 'Is he okay? He seemed fine this morning.'

Cam frowned and considered his boots. 'He didn't say?' Adele shook her head. 'Well, yeah, occasionally he does too much, you know?' And he swivelled on the spot away from her, the conversation over.

Adele hoped Blake was okay, but this was business and she still had to pull off the best wedding ever. As if she could forget, and these few days beforehand were equally important. 'And you're acquainted with Kingsley Estate wines?'

Cam broke into a wide, open smile, showing off yellowed teeth. 'Yeah, I've been around these parts for years and worked with Blake since he took over the place. I help out.'

*He helps out?* Picking up a cloth, Adele scoured the top of the already clean bar with hurried strokes, before dropping the sponge into the sink and scrubbing her hands with super-hot water.

'Um, well, that's great. Blake must appreciate your help. But this tasting needs to go well, like super well.' *Otherwise this family will hate me and this wedding!* 'So, is there like a list of tasting notes that we can refer to. I can assist.' She reefed out each drawer and slammed it back in its place with little success.

'Adele.' Cam touched her arm. His words were kind and soft, like a grandfather. 'I'm not a repair man, I'm the wine consultant. When Blake bought the place, he didn't know much about the growing of vines or the production of wine. I've grown grapes for more than three decades, and at this vineyard for the last five years. You're in good hands.'

Her body sagged with relief, and she let go of the drawer handle she was clutching. 'Okay, great, thank you. Let me know whatever you'd like me to do.'

The family filed in. A small compact group comprising Juliette's parents and sister, two friends that would be bridesmaids and two pairs of aunts and uncles. Luke's family and friends would make up the balance of guests, but they weren't arriving until Saturday.

'Where are Luke and Juliette?' she asked the sister, Clare.

Clare was young and meticulously groomed. '*Preparation de mariage* or how you say, wedding preparation.' She shrugged.

No way! She was doing everything. Her mind whizzed with thoughts. Should she search for them or leave them be? The image of what they might be doing made her stomach swirl. But then, Cam commandeered the room with a bold, assuring voice, and she was swept away with his talk of tannins, notes, sweetness and acidity.

Cam gave a spiel about the Estate and its history. The Hamilton family owned it before they retired and Blake Kingsley had taken over, rebranded and revitalised the vineyard. In his words, taken it to a whole new level. Wow, Blake was doing well, then. Adele was continuously impressed by him.

The family grew restless and started reaching for the bottles. Cam was fast on his feet and intervened to serve them. The first on the tasting list was a chardonnay. He poured and drew the family's attention back to him.

Adele wasn't a big fan of wine but she sipped the golden liquid too. Her mouth burst with the flavour of peach and melon followed by an unpleasant woody after-taste. Reluctantly, she swallowed the remainder. She had to set the example, didn't she?

The family sipped their own tasters and spat the remnants into the little steel barrels sitting on each table. Argh! This is why she avoided wine tastings. Her stomach roiled at the sight of the liquid spurting from their mouths.

'Not a fan of wine tasting, hey?' Cam was beside her.

She hadn't loved the chardonnay either, but there was hardly any need for the dramatic display of expelling it from their mouths. 'I didn't think the wine was that bad...'

Cam laughed. 'There's no offense, it's best to take a little sip, roll the wine around your mouth and spit out the residue.'

Yep, gross.

Between the first three varieties, the guests cleansed their palette with a variety of high-quality cheese and crackers. There was a lot of French chatter, loud and fast and Adele couldn't decipher if that was a good or a bad thing. There were quite a few hand gestures, as well. No smiles, though.

Next up was the signature Verdelho. Having learned his lesson, Cam poured as he talked. Adele followed his lead and swirled the liquid, placed her nose deep in the glass and then took a first, tiny sip. Cam said Blake had taken a risk. Chardonnay was the common and most accepted wine produced in the region. But he wanted Verdelho and had worked hard in those beginning years, against opposition, to develop his perfect Verdelho vines. Now, his dream had been realised. Cam didn't take any of the credit.

She was getting the hang of this. 'It smells like fruit salad,' she said loud enough for the group to hear.

Cam laughed. 'Yes, that's right. You have a good nose.' Adele instinctively touched her face. 'But yes, Verdelho is famous for its tropical, dry fresh taste.'

Adele tried it. 'Oh, that's delicious!'

'I'm glad you think so.' A body slid onto the stool beside her, her nerve endings came alive and she knew, immediately, it was Blake. His voice was deep and husky like he'd just risen from a deep slumber. Turning, there he was, devilishly handsome and wearing his wide and authentic smile. Heat suffused her neck. Blake accepted a glass from Cam with a slap to his back. Adele caught the look exchanged between them.

'What about champagne?' Clare asked.

'No champagne or sparkling at this vineyard.'

The women erupted in outrage. 'There must be champagne at a wedding!' The mother of the bride exclaimed. 'We should have brought our own!' Her accent was clipped.

'Oh, no, no. No need,' Adele jumped from her seat. How had she missed this vital detail? 'I have ordered some especially for the wedding, of course.' She swivelled to Blake, her eyebrows arching towards her forehead in question. Blake nodded in understanding.

Just as fast she spun back. 'So, you see, no need to worry.'

'What about the red wine then? We love our red wine.'

'Well, you are in the right place,' Cam continued, unperturbed. 'We have some excellent quality cabernet sauvignon.' A groan erupted from one of the uncles seated at the rear of the room. 'And a merlot, if you prefer,' Cam continued.

'Yes, let's try some of both.' Adele rose, collected a bottle from Cam and filled the glasses. The satisfaction of the serving size cheered the family and feeling jubilant, she poured herself one, too. At the last moment, Blake stole her glass away and wine spilled onto the table, spreading like blood across the white cloth. Hands fast, Blake stymied the spill with a napkin and handed her a clean glass.

'You can't mix the wines,' he said. Adele nodded, inspecting the tumbler for cleanliness and diverted her gaze from the red-soaked table. Urgh! She sat, and without bothering to appreciate the scent or allow it to air, she drank the blood red liquid straight down. Blake sipped his Verdelho.

It was silky and smooth and propelled through her veins, offering an immediate calming effect. Around her, though, she sensed disquiet. Without glancing at Blake, she rose again and refilled empty glasses. One of the uncles, she couldn't remember his name, Paul, Pierre, Peter...spat his Merlo into the bucket, his face scrunched up as if it was repulsive. She smelled strong cherry and plum and traced the liquid in the container as it raced around the rim. Then the man popped a slice of cheese into his mouth, licked his fingers and reached for an olive.

A light sheen of perspiration gathered on Adele's skin. Feeling suddenly light-headed, the bottle she held slipped through her fingers, smashing to the ground. Red wine splattered onto her legs, over her feet and across the floor.

It was the contamination of germs. From his mouth to the

platter, to the floor, to her body. It was too much. Through watery eyes she searched for her bag, her feet yet to move. Now the man sniffled. Was he sick? More germs! Urgh, she was in hell. Fleeing to the sink, she ran the hot tap and scrubbed her hands until they burned. Yanking open a cupboard door, she found a cloth and rushed back. She'd clean everything until it gleamed; any bacteria wouldn't stand a chance. But Blake stood in her path.

'*What is she doing?*' one of the guests exclaimed.

Cam and Blake book-ended her. 'Leave it Adele, I'll clean up. There's broken glass and we don't want anyone getting hurt.' Blake directed her to the stool while Cam ushered the family out, the quintessential professional and professing his thanks at their enjoyment and attention.

The large, timber double-barrelled door slammed shut.

'Urgh! That was an absolute disaster. The family hated it and,' she dropped her voice an octave, 'were so rude. I'm sorry, Blake, they hated your wines.' She jumped up. 'I should go after them, fix this, see what else they'd like to do.'

Blake tugged her back down. 'No. They're adults responsible for their behaviour and can sort out their own entertainment this afternoon.'

'I'm so sorry,' she repeated and hung her head in her hands.

'What for? It's not your fault.'

'The wine tasting was a disaster. Luke will be mad.'

Blake grabbed fresh glasses from behind the bar and moved around the tables. He collected one untouched platter and placed it in front of Adele; her eyes bulged.

'What is it with you and this,' he struggled for words, 'this cleaning hands, wiping down benches, disinfectant and sanitising. I notice you have two showers a day, too.'

'Usually more, but I'm too polite staying with you to do that.'

Now his eyes shot toward his forehead, but she remained silent.

'And as for Luke, firstly, he didn't show so cannot complain, and secondly, he's getting married for nix at my place and his best friend is organising the entire shindig, I'm also guessing gravitas.'

'My phobia to germs drives him crazy.'

'Sorry to interrupt, you two. Letting you know all is safe and clean and back to normal...' Adele went to interrupt Cam, but he held up a flat palm. 'No apologies necessary, that was a tough audience. I'll leave you to it, I'm off to fix the far fence so those attacking alpacas don't get out!' He chuckled and left with a wave.

'You told him!' She play punched Blake on the arm.

'He's my right-hand man, my friend.' Blake's voice was low and sounding sentimental.

'He seems like a great guy.'

'Yeah, he is. But back to the germs...I mean we all have our foibles, I like to exercise a lot, drink a lot...'

'Get a lot of headaches...'

The words hung in the sizzling air between them. Blake hung his head. 'Yep, a lot of headaches, but germs hey. You don't like them?'

'Gosh, it's way more than that.' He cracked a smile, putting her at ease. 'When I was little, my mum got really sick and almost died. Had a staph infection that led to sepsis after having an open wound. I was ten and all I remember is the hospital and the strict rules about cleaning and the eradication of germs to avoid risk of further infection. To a kid the sterile environment was frightening. But what I took away from that was the importance of being clean and avoiding germs. If you are clean, you don't get sick. Ever since, I've been fanatical about hygiene.'

'Have you seen anyone about it?'

'Oh, yeah, for sure. I've been checked out. It's considered an obsession and compulsion, but it doesn't affect my lifestyle, you know, my quality of life. They say it's also related to being a perfectionist and a more methodical and organised person. I mean, if you have those tendencies you're more likely to develop these sorts of compulsions. It doesn't stop me from doing things and that's why I've never been diagnosed with OCD. If you can believe it, I'm not that bad.' She smiled making light of the pain and heartache of a life of constant worry about bugs.

'Well, it's timely right, with the pandemic and all. There's a profound greater need now to demonstrate good hygiene.' His lips curled into a smile. 'I'm not making fun of you, it sounds sort of heavy, is there anything I can do?'

Blake poured them both a drink and ate some cheese.

She shook her head, her hair fanning her face, her eyes watering.

'And as for the wedding and the family, it's going to be great. You're putting in so much work and Luke should be grateful.'

He placed his hand on her arm. It was instinctive, like you'd offer comfort to a friend, but he quickly realised his gaffe and removed it. But those few seconds of his touch, and heat reverberated straight to her core. And most definitely made her forget all about possible contamination.

'It has to be perfect.'

Blake's eyebrows knitted together making his eyes squint.

He was about to say something...

'This is your true love, is it?' And she held up the glass of Verdelho.

His features changed into something hard to read. Astonishment? Surprise? Perhaps realisation.

'I think you're right. The only lady I can rely upon.' He gazed at the glass in adoration. 'I've entered her into a prestigious wine competition. I think she'll go okay. She's good even though the big winery producers mock us out here in the granite belt. I'll show them, if not this year, then another. But this vintage is one of the best I've produced.'

He held his glass aloft and gazed at the pale liquid, proud of his achievement. Why didn't Blake have someone special in his life? Her heart was melting little by little at this conversation. He was kind, gentle, attentive and respectful, certainly towards her. A niggle at the back of her head made the inevitable comparison to his brother. Luke rarely had time for her, was more selfish in his pursuits and tended to mock the softer, more sensitive qualities of other people. Luke might be insecure, but he had other admirable qualities.

'Well, you might just convert me to being a wine snob. I love this, it's delicious. Congratulations.'

'WHERE'S MY DRINK?' IN THE SEAT BESIDE HIM, ADELE'S BACK went ramrod straight and she brushed down imaginary and wayward loose strands of hair on her head.

Luke appeared behind them, one hand on each of their shoulder's. His eyes skittered over the empty bottles of wine and the plates of food on the table.

Adele and Blake still sat in the cellar door, hours after Juliette's family had left. Time had passed quickly, and the more wine they'd consumed, the more they'd laughed and shared. A warm glow passed through Blake, and it wasn't from his fabulous wine.

'Adele was right in the middle of the story of how you met.'

'Ah, the semi-formal story. That's getting a bit old, isn't it?' Luke reached over and found a bottle with a residue of wine left and poured it into a dirty glass. Blake noticed Adele's shiver.

'Aw, don't say that,' Adele crooned. Her glassy eyes were sparkling in Luke's direction. 'It's a great story, marking the beginning of our friendship. It was fate, a chance meeting and we've been inseparable ever since.'

'Ain't that true, bestie.' Luke flashed a seductive grin. Adele came alive, blossoming next to him, whereas a sinking feeling deposited itself in his gut. He'd observed Adele to be whip smart, funny, dedicated to her job, kind and caring and yet she responded to the juvenile charm of his brother. It didn't quite make sense to him, and he didn't want to stereotype her to be like every other woman, and yet...

'Where were you? You didn't come to the wine tasting!' Adele accused, laughing, her tease light and buttery.

Blake rose. He couldn't stand by and watch the banter back and forth between the two. 'I better head up to the restaurant and check on things. Thanks for the chat this afternoon, Adele, and for the company and the wine tasting. Really, you did a great job.'

She offered him a smile of thanks and shifted on the stool, almost losing her balance. Both men reached out to prevent her fall. 'I've got her bro,' Luke said, and Blake left.

# 6

*Thursday: three days before the wedding*

Adele swung the door open to Blake's quarters without knocking. She'd moved into her own cabin last night as the Estate emptied of its guests. Her cabin was warm, inviting and comfortable in true country style, but she'd scored the most distant cottage down the back and it was a trek to the homestead. She arrived puffing from the exertion.

It had been strange sleeping alone, in the quiet, only the noises of the outback for company. Nice, but weird, especially after sharing Blake's tiny apartment where she could hear his every move and take comfort in the fact he was nearby. Was it only four days ago that they'd slept together and she'd barged in on him in the shower? Her body warmed at the memories.

'Hello!' The dogs rushed at her down the narrow hall and she paused to greet them. There was no answer from Blake.

Darn, she might be too late, perhaps he'd already left for the day? Adele searched the apartment until she spotted his large feet sticking out behind the couch. 'Hello,' she repeated. No response. Moving closer, she saw Blake was lying on the living room floor with his eyes closed. 'Oh, Blake. Are you okay? Blake?' Wracking her brain she tried to remember basic first aid. She knelt and felt his pulse; it beat in his neck and she released a puff of air. She shook his shoulders, gently, then more robust. His eyes blinked open, once, twice. 'Blake, Blake. Are you okay? What's wrong?'

He came around, dazed but conscious. Grasping under his shoulders, she sagged. Gosh, he was a solid weight. Lifting again, she half-dragged him until his back rested against the couch, legs stretched out in front.

'Hey,' she waved her hand in front of his face.

Not startled by her sudden appearance, his head turned in slow motion and his eyes blinked in succession.

'Are you okay? What's wrong?'

Moments passed and she waited as he returned from some other place to the present.

'Um, yeah, I'm fine. A bad migraine. I've been vomiting most of the night. Haven't slept much but must have crashed out, exhausted.'

Adele felt his forehead. It was clammy and hot, his face pale. 'You look awful.'

'Thanks.' And his lips cracked into a tight smile.

'You sure do get some serious headaches. Have you eaten? What can I do?'

'Coffee, please,' he croaked.

'Coffee? No, seriously? That can't be good for you. You must be dehydrated from vomiting.'

'Actually, it's one of the remedies. Drinking caffeine helps to alleviate the pain and enhances the effect of the medication I take.' She stared at him trying to decipher if he was telling the truth.

'No, it's true. Do you think I'd honestly drink it if it made me feel worse?'

'Should I get the doctor, or should we go to hospital?'

Blake shook his head, but it must have pained him as he grimaced. 'Nothing they can do. I've got the drugs and I have to sit it out. The pain goes away, it always does, eventually.'

'Okay, don't move. I'll get coffee and water.' She touched his shoulder before moving to the kitchen.

Delivering two coffees moments later, she sat on the floor next to him.

On the low table in front lay an open scrap book.

'What's this?' Inside were magazine articles and clippings and photographs. Blake didn't reply.

'Is this you?' Adele flicked the pages in quick succession. 'Blake, this is incredible. I wondered if you'd played, but you never said anything.'

He watched her now and gave a slight shrug. 'Don't talk about it anymore, no point.' He indicated to one piece. 'That's me in the local rag when I was first drafted. My mum started this album, kept every news article, every photo.'

Adele's stomach sank and she flipped to the end. The last date was more than five years ago. She closed the book.

'What happened?'

He stared at her long and hard. 'The headaches...'

She murmured in encouragement, hoping he continued.

'Well, you're a fan. You know it's a tough sport. I was good, played hard, got best and fairest a few years in a row. But playing hard comes at a price. I was knocked out many times, too many, as it turns out.' His gaze went to the window then. 'There's headaches, the inability to sleep, and some memory loss; it all relates to the concussions and head injuries I suffered. It's a thing. I had to stop playing and can only hope now that I stopped soon enough and the condition doesn't deteriorate.'

'I'm so sorry. It must be a dreadful loss.'

'I miss it,' his voice cracked. 'Not just the game. Football was my entire life. But also, my wife was used to me being this big, celebrity football star, until I wasn't. My life fell apart.'

His wife?

'I know saying sorry doesn't help, but I am. I'm sorry this happened to you. It's really shitty. And the ongoing symptoms, that's tough.'

'That's why I have the Estate and vineyard. My new project and life.'

'And the dogs and those attacking alpacas!' They laughed together, gentle, uncertain. Her heart rate finally returned to normal.

They sipped their coffee in silent solidarity. There were a million things to ask, but she didn't. Except one...

'Please reassure me that you're under the best medical care?'

'Yes.' Adele waited for further explanation, but Blake didn't elaborate. Sensing he didn't want to talk about it anymore, she didn't push. In fact, he didn't speak but sipped the coffee and continued to gaze out the window.

It was a beautiful morning; those glorious first few hours where the world was waking up, the birds leaving their nests, the dew on the grass evaporating and the sun rising high in the sky.

She'd arrived early to discuss the day's activity. But she couldn't talk about that now. Not after finding Blake unwell, not after his revelation. Her issues were trivial in comparison.

Nonetheless, she had work to do. Today the family were having an exclusive experience with the alpacas. After the disaster of yesterday, she woke up sweating and worried. So many things could go wrong with the wild animals and the picnic they'd planned. Blake had been instrumental in helping her organise the experience and she knew he'd calm her.

Except, for once, he couldn't. It was heartbreaking to see someone usually so alive, always active, suddenly still. If Blake wasn't working the vines, he'd be shooting hoops or running or chasing the dogs. But now, well, it made more sense. And all she wanted to do was help him, make it better.

Marshmallow whined at her feet and crawled onto Blake's lap. A tiny smile formed on his lips.

Anyway, she was being silly about the schedule. Every detail was planned, of course, but it was the unexpected contingencies she feared the most. Nothing unpredictable would happen...would it?

'Is there anything I can do?' Again, his head turned in her direction as if he moved under water.

But then there was a spark. 'Yes. Can you feed the dogs? I haven't done it yet.' She listened to the instructions. 'I'll have a shower and be across to organise the alpacas. It'll be a great morning.'

Did he sense her anxiety? Wouldn't be hard, she figured.

'Okay, only if you're up to it.' She crooned at Marshmallow. 'See you in a bit.'

'OH, WOW, THANK GOODNESS.' ADELE'S SPIRITS SOARED AT THE idyllic scene.

A herd of alpacas roamed inside the fenced area while others were led on long ropes and all were perfectly well-behaved. As were the guests! Maybe today was the day and everyone would enjoy this special event she'd arranged.

Maybe this could still be the best wedding ever!

Blake was on the far side feeding an alpaca while a small group of children watched. The big hulk of man that was him, kneeled at child height, and laughed, his head thrown back. A warm glow spread through her chest at the sight of him up and moving, acting more like himself. It was like the sun had suddenly appeared from behind a grey cloud.

Her eyes scanned the rest of the group...and that warmness dissipated like a heavy downpour of rain arriving unexpectedly. Luke and Juliette were here today, that was something for small mercies, the event was for them, but... they were kissing. Passionately. Her eyes widened as an alpaca advanced towards them. Oblivious, Luke had one hand on Juliette's hip, the other at the base of her neck, their bodies aligned... but so much more... an ache shot through her chest.

A black mass of fur nudged Luke's back. He batted it away. Being ignored didn't suit the alpaca and it shoved again and Luke struck out with his flat palm. 'Oh!' Adele covered her mouth with her hand. Okay, she agreed they were attacking alpacas, but she'd never go so far as to hurt one. Damnit, she didn't want to crawl through the fence and go over there. But the alpaca bounced on its toes back and forth, its tail flicking. A quick glance at Blake and she ascertained he was no help as he continued to chat with the children.

Once successfully through the fence without touching it, she zig-zagged left and right to avoid wandering alpacas and was almost at Luke when the animal reared back and spat in Juliette's face.

Juliette screamed. That caught Blake's attention. He handed his reins over to Cam who stood nearby and fled across the field. Adele hesitated; her feet stationary as if they were stuck in mud. She gripped her stomach as if that would prevent its swooping and bowed her head. No, not today. Bloody alpacas! This was her fault because she was late due to Uncle Frederick having had too much to drink last night and requiring an urgent hangover remedy. Plus, she'd had to field calls from Lily, worried that the chosen white flowers would not be available and that was before she'd had to apply recovery cream to Clare's sunburn.

All in the day's work of the wedding planner. But rescuing the bride from an attacking alpaca was not on her agenda today.

Taking deep breaths, she made her feet move, one step after the other while rummaging in her bag for the multiple bottles of sanitiser and wipes she had stored. Arriving, Blake's tone was light, making fun of the situation; Juliette's was dire. Her face like thunder. Blake's smile dropped.

She'd fix it, she had too. Reaching Juliette, she dabbed at her face with the moist cloth until the wipe was stained brown with make-up. Juliette batted Adele's hand away and the dirty material dropped to the dirt from the sting of the contact.

'Honestly, Pancake only wanted your attention. No harm done. Adele's been spat on before haven't you, Adele?'

Yes, and it was the grossest thing she's ever experienced, but she didn't utter those words. Instead, she offered a tight smile, not exactly sure what would smooth over this debacle. Meanwhile, Luke caressed his fiancé's arm and offered reassurances. The offending alpaca wasn't at all disturbed and enjoyed the neck rub Blake offered.

'Let's get you cleaned up because there's a whole day of activities you don't want to miss. Your family is enjoying getting to know the other animals. This one is clearly too frisky.' Her tone was high pitched, and Blake glanced at her with an odd expression. 'After this there's paint and sip with the alpacas and we have the picnic lunch planned with photographs this afternoon as well.'

Juliette scowled and stormed off, Luke on her tail.

Adele turned to Blake. 'Your bloody alpacas are trouble!' She said it with a broad smile but only because Blake had the animal in a headlock and under control. 'Are you feeling better?' she added.

'Yes, thanks.' His expression turned serious for a moment before he recovered. 'And,' now his grin spread wide across his face and his cheeks creased, 'my alpacas are the best. They sense an easy target. And don't like being ignored. I mean if you want to snog, go somewhere private. This area belongs to the alpacas and they expect people to give them attention.'

'Right, so it's all the human's fault?'

'Yep, absolutely.' Blake laughed and a funny little fizzle went off in her tummy. She turned away.

Adele's teeth worried her bottom lip as her gaze followed the disappearing pair. 'I should go after them.' Pancake nuzzled under her arm forcing his head up and against her chest, his face close to her cheek. She stiffened, bracing for the worst, but the animal only leaned against her side. She shut her eyes.

Blake placed a reassuring hand to her back. 'Alpacas are very clean, you know. They don't smell. Inhale, you won't detect a bad scent and they are hygienic in their habits, especially where they go to the toilet. Unlike livestock who go anywhere, even dogs, alpacas are so clean they only poo in one or two areas.'

Adele peeked one eye open to stare at him. 'You think talking about alpaca poo helps right now? Its tongue was probably licking it balls right before touching my face!'

Blake hugged Pancake around its long neck. 'Aw, Pancake is a beautiful girl and would never dream of groping someone else's balls.' He talked in his sing-song happy voice designed for animals and children. The animal soaked up the attention while Adele searched for her bag.

Blake gripped her forearm, stilling her frantic movements. 'You can clean your hands in a minute. We have a tap and soap over there especially for guests. For a few minutes, stand still, give her a pet.' Blake reached for her hand; his was warm and a nice mixture of smooth and work rough. He guided it to Pancake's neck before gliding it up and down.

'Is she crooning?' Adele said, wonder having crept into her voice, even if her hand was shaking.

'See, Pancake's a good 'un, she likes you!'

Adele tolerated the feel of the fluffy, crimpy fleece before taking one step back as a shiver raced up her spine. 'Okay, that's enough,' and she held her hands out in front of her lest those germs invade the rest of her body.

'Listen,' his fingers traced the bare skin on her arm for the briefest moment before he removed it, letting it hang back by his side. 'Juliette will be fine. You know the spray doesn't hurt, it's basically water, so leave them be. Hopefully Juliette will clean up and they'll come back.'

Adele frowned.

'I promise I'll help you. We're in this together. I'll do my best to control the attacking alpacas and help you set up.' Taking in the surrounds, he said further, 'everything is under control at the moment. Let's give them another fifteen minutes and we'll set up the painting equipment. That'll be a nice lead into lunch.'

She'd accept Blake's help. Anything to make this wedding wonderful. 'Okay, thank you, you're the best.' Blake's eyes smouldered in her direction; the heat hit her neck first before the blush must have turned her cheeks rouge. 'Let's do it,' she said but her words were soft and croaky.

BLAKE APPROACHED ADELE ON THE BANKS OF THE CREEK THAT crept its way across his Estate. The flowing stream was a calming, constant presence that attracted wildlife and encouraged deep green shrubbery and foliage to grow. A perfect spot for the planned picnic.

'This looks incredible, you've done such a great job,' he said arriving at her side. She'd changed into a halter-neck summer dress that kept her shoulders bare. The afternoon light revealed a scattering of light freckles. The gold-toned colour of the dress should have clashed with those flashes of pink in her hair, but it didn't. His breath caught at her beauty. Her innocence. But, hold up, he'd forgotten himself. Women weren't innocent or unassuming. In his experience, they were calculating and with set agendas to get what they wanted. No, that wasn't fair. His intelligent mind knew not all women were like his ex-wife, or shared the characteristics of his philandering father, but his heart waivered on that fact. Unfortunately, thinking the worst had become his default position.

Something he needed to change. Adele appeared different, but could he trust his instincts? Thinking about her brought back memories of their night together and her naked body beneath him...

No mistaking the fact that he missed her around his place: her soft voice and fresh feminine scent that clung to the air. It still lingered on his pillow.

'Oh, you're the sweetest. I've never had so many compliments before.' Adele was speaking to him, and he zeroed back into the present.

'No, seriously, it looks like a scene out of one of those glossy magazines. You've really got a knack.'

'Now you're going too far. I've borrowed most of this stuff from you. People must love the picnic option you offer.' She paused and looked around her. 'It's so beautiful here, romantic.' Did she sigh? 'The gurgling creek, the scenery, the animals, vines nearby, idyllic. You must love it.'

'I do. And people love the picnics, but we don't set it up like this for them. No crystal glasses and silverware. They collect their basket and blanket and find a spot. What you've done is special, oh, and the flowers, nice touch.'

Adele kept making minor changes to the set out. 'How is the paint and sip going?'

Blake paused. 'Well, I've never seen a group attend paint and sip and not actually paint. That is the point, however...' Adele was about to break in and interrupt. He held up his hand in a 'hold it' gesture. 'They're drinking the wines they criticised yesterday and being entertained by an eight-year-old birthday party, so, overall, it's a success.'

Adele's brow furrowed deeper and between her eyes creased. Her sign of worry. It was funny how quickly you could get to know someone...

'Usually during the picnics, we let the alpaca wander around close by, but today, I think we'll tether them to the fence. Do you agree?'

'Yes!' And they twirled around to see Luke and Juliette approach.

'I'll go and fetch the rest of the family,' Blake addressed Adele but she was fixated on the couple. Her smile was lopsided, and her head tilted to the left in a whimsical fashion until a mask of reserve flashed across her features, replacing whatever emotion she hid. Luke and Juliette were oblivious to her as they strode hand-in-hand. But then, Blake caught the dart of Luke's eyes to the left, taking in Adele, before he once again focused on Juliette. He exaggerated his attention to his bride then. Adele's shoulders sagged. As he walked away, they were engaged in conversation, Adele appearing strained.

Upon his return, the family made a fuss over the couple, now seated on the blanket closest to the stream, gurgling water their background music as Adele poured their drinks. She was the wedding planner and not the servant and discomfort unfurled in his stomach. Was it because she was serving them or was it something else?

Swiping a bottle of champagne, Blake checked the label and was satisfied it was worth drinking. Adele had chosen well. He poured a generous portion into a flute.

'Adele,' he grasped her at the elbow, indicated to the drink. 'Let's leave the lovebirds alone and have a drink.'

Luke stopped pawing his future wife. 'Are you trying to steal my best friend, mate?' Luke leaned onto his elbow. 'What about your footy friends? Where are they these days? Oh, that's right, they're hanging out with your wife.'

Adele went pale.

Blake swallowed. Banter between him and Luke wasn't unusual, that usual brother-type of one upmanship. In their younger years there had been significant rivalry between them, which was sort of ridiculous given they were two very different men. But Blake understood it was about attention and Blake had always received the notoriety and Luke had hated it. He had been in the press often and the girls flocked to him like he was a star. When the good times were good, they were really good and Luke had faded into the background, a place he never liked.

'Adele, has Blake told you about his wife?'

Blake was used to backhanded sneers and comments, they'd been thick and fast in his playing day; most of the time he ignored them. This was personal, though, and his brother was out of line. Should he ignore it or make a scene? Adele banked on the day's events going well and was stressed about the picnic, so he'd let things go, this time.

'Adele's been working hard, she might like a break.' Adele flashed him a smile in thanks, and paused.

'Let's have that drink,' he encouraged and nodded towards a spare picnic blanket. Thankfully she followed and quickly regained some colour.

'Are you still married?' she asked before they were both seated on the plaid rug.

'No. We divorced twelve months after she left me.'

'That was cruel of Luke. Does he know the real reason you split?'

Blake laughed, hollow and low. 'Yes, but it's convenient to forget. He hated the attention I received playing footy. I guess a fair bit of that sibling rivalry remains. Perhaps he's jealous we're spending time together.'

Her face blanched again. 'Did you tell him about us?'

Blake paused. 'No, but would it matter?'

She replied with a simple shrug before sipping her drink and casting a glance around her. Always working. He was getting to know her more each day but knew little of what made her tick.

Yeah, his attraction to her was growing... He was dreaming of the smooth skin under her dress when Adele spoke.

'Tell me about your wife.' Her smile was nervous, tentative and she glanced across to Luke. Blake turned in that direction to see Luke watching them. Adele scooted back on the rug, increasing her distance.

He hung his head. Was this really about his wife?

'There's not much to say.' That was an understatement. 'I loved her and she left me for my best friend.'

'Oh,' now her hand palmed his, but only for a moment. 'I'm so sorry, that's terrible.'

He shrugged now which didn't in any way sum up his feelings about the matter.

'Are you still friends with your mate?'

'No. He was another player on the team...'

A shriek went up behind them. An alpaca had escaped its tethering and was munching the picnic food at Juliette's parent's blanket, much to their great horror.

'Another attacking alpaca,' Adele said but only to him and with a smile, lighting up her face. 'I told you, these animals are trouble and you clearly can't control them!' They both jumped up.

'Are you going to rescue the family and drag away the naughty animal?' he joked with a glint in his eye.

She returned it. 'I will stand by and assist the family and ensure that you, owner and operator of the alpaca farm, safely escort the beast to time out for his misbehaviour.'

Blake saluted in obeyance. Before he raced away, she placed her arm on his. 'I'm sorry about your wife. Betrayal must hurt. Let's continue our talk, okay?' A small flicker of something ignited low in his stomach. But keeping with the light-hearted nature of their conversation, he agreed. 'Tonight, my room?' and he offered her what he knew wasn't the sexy and inviting grin he'd been trying to emulate. It was probably more bashful and hopeful. Before she could answer, there was another cry and they turned to face the alpaca who had a scone in its mouth and was wearing a jam and cream moustache. Adele laughed and shoved Blake in the back to save the day.

ADELE FLICKED THE SWITCH ON THE KETTLE FOR THE THIRD TIME. 'Damnit! I'm going to make the stupid tea.'

She poured two mugs of chamomile, leaving the bags in to steep, carried one in each hand and left the cabin. Tiny lantern-shaped garden lights guided Adele along the path back towards the homestead.

For the past hour she'd been tossing up whether Blake's offer had been genuine or said in jest? Should she go and say hi and offer him an herbal tea? It might help him sleep and perhaps reduce the prospect of a headache in the morning. Who knew the power of natural remedies, right?

She wasn't usually indecisive but had changed her mind so many times she'd lost count and was now suitably frustrated with herself. Only days ago they'd been sharing cramped quarters and seeing each other naked, surely she can make the man a cup of tea!

No turning back now, she was on her way and hoped that he was still awake.

'Is that an Uber delivery for me?' A voice came out of the darkness.

It was the familiar and husky voice she loved, and she turned towards Luke seated on his deck where he was swallowed by the darkness. Adele cast a furtive glance in the direction of the homestead, feeling torn in two directions. What was Blake doing? Was his head aching again or was he finally, blissfully asleep?

Luke must have sensed her hesitation. And it was a first for her. Hesitating about Luke? 'Well?' His tone was impatient. She'd spent years acquiescing to his every request, laughing at his every joke, playing taxi, being available for him at short notice, and yet, Adele wasn't stupid. When her attention was diverted elsewhere and for the briefest moment, she put aside her devotion to him, Luke'd pull out all stops and pamper her with a special day, take her to the races, treat her like a princess, or simply as a friend should. Did Luke have some uncanny sense that her interest was captured elsewhere? That perhaps she had a new friend? And Blake was a friend...but there was that little niggle, deep down inside of her that wondered if it could be something else. What? She had no idea. She had not opened her heart to the prospect of anyone but Luke for years, so how would she recognise the signs?

And plus, her best friend was about to get married. Thus far, none of her charms had worked, despite her efforts to produce the best wedding ever. It was almost laughable, almost!

'C'mon, Ad, come and sit with me. I'm getting married in two days, who knows when we'll get to hang out again.' He patted the seat beside him.

Would she go to him? Of course, she would, there'd really never been a choice. Perhaps after he was married and ultimately didn't choose her, she might get on with her life.

She trod up the three short stairs and handed him the tea.

BLAKE SAT ON HIS BOTTOM STEP WHILE MARSHMALLOW AND THE other dogs went out before bed. He laughed as they chased their tails and other invisible things in the night.

His gaze flicked up to the back corner, the far cabin. The lights were illuminated and his mind filled Adele. He'd given up waiting for her. His invitation was sort of a joke, after all. Obviously, she had better things to do. Maybe some last-minute wedding plans? Assisting other clients? She had an incredible work ethic and never stopped. Or was that only for Luke?

He knew the pair were friends but sometimes when he watched them together, it seemed more than that, the air around them grew loaded. And what were those wisecracks today? Luke jumping in to stake his territory? Adele must have other friends.

The dogs paused, their tails pointed and barked in that

direction. It was a good few hundred metres away, but he heard it too. Voices.

Blake could just make out a figure on the path illuminated by the dim lights. He couldn't detect any detail but it was the determined pace and step that gave it away as Adele. She paused in front of Luke's cabin. He couldn't hear the words but there was talking and then she veered off track and was lost to the darkness. A late night call? As usual, his mind went in all the wrong directions. Surely not? Luke was about to get married. Blake hung his head, unfortunately he wouldn't put such antics past his brother. He loved his brother, but well, he wasn't always the nicest bloke, and had never been able to shake that chip that sat on his shoulder. But Adele? He shouldn't find that hard to believe, either. And yet, disappointment made his shoulders heavy.

Sitting outside in the big, wide-open world, the stars shining like diamonds in the sky, life was good. His team had won their preliminary game tonight and were off to the finals next week. Had Adele watched? Did she know?

He didn't want to always think the worst, but he could thank his unfaithful ex-wife for that gift. God, he'd loved her, fiercely with his entire heart, and then some. Way more than he'd ever loved his footy and that said a lot. Unfortunately, those feelings weren't reciprocated when things got tough. When their lives changed because of his injury Lisa couldn't hack it, it wasn't the life she signed up for, she said. Well, he hadn't signed up for it either, but there was no exit option for him. Lucky Lisa.

An ache tore through his chest. But that was more likely the pain of failure, still beating strong, even now, all these years later.

Perhaps if she'd simply left him, that would have been okay.

But to leave him for his teammate? Low blow by anyone's standards.

The talking receded and Blake didn't want to dwell on what the two of them might be doing. Did it matter? It was none of his business. But he couldn't dislodge the twist in his gut.

## 7

_Friday: day before the wedding_

The family walked outside in single file. Adele's breath caught in her throat and her heart pounded. Until she saw it; the arch of an eyebrow, eyes widening and smiles blossoming. Sentences spoken in fast and fluent French. Adele didn't need to know the words to translate the universal language of happiness, wonder and enchantment.

Bingo.

She'd done it again. A tingle of excitement raced through her. Would this be the moment? Would the extensive effort she'd undertaken to coordinate the rehearsal dinner be enough to make Luke realise? Would it finally happen?

Tonight's setting was outside, the same location as the reception tomorrow. Except tomorrow was Australiana and modern and elegant; tonight was fun and in honour of the French heritage of the bride. The outdoor area situated between the homestead and the vines was lit by a deep blue hue on all sides with small, delicate fairy lights interspersed to create a sprinkling of white amongst the blue. The tables were adorned with mini–Eiffel Towers and bright red roses, gerberas and chrysanthemums in-between. The serviettes were white cloth, finishing the red, white and blue theme of their home country. The chairs for the bride and groom were labelled with the words 'Monsieur' and 'Madame' respectively. Her idea; the concept could have been tacky, could have turned out terribly, but it didn't. Under anyone else, it may have been a disaster, but with Adele as organiser, it was perfect.

The red carpet was in position leading to the gazebo. At the head was an old rustic bicycle decorated in more blooms, releasing an intoxicating scent. Tomorrow the bike would be transformed to the white and green preference of Juliette. Tonight, it was decorated in bright colours.

Adele soaked up the accolades even if they weren't shouted in her direction. Juliette smiled at her family, not at Adele. At least the bride was happy, even if she didn't acknowledge the effort it had taken to prepare this grand setting.

Luke made up for it. 'This looks incredible, thank you,' and he kissed her on the cheek causing her body to tingle.

'Okay, now everyone is here. Let's practice the ceremony.'

He pulled back, took a hefty swig of his beer. 'Nah, it'll be perfect, don't worry.'

Unsure, Adele turned to Juliette, who ignored her and continued talking with her mother.

Okay. That was the whole point of the rehearsal dinner, right? But hey, whatever the bride and groom wanted. She'd rest easier if they practiced, but she'd be on hand to direct and guide tomorrow, anyway. The schedule was etched into her brain.

Adele sat down next to Blake. Usually, she was not a guest at the dinner, and never at the reception, but she played dual roles at this wedding: planner and friend. Blake offered a tight smile; they hadn't crossed paths all day.

'Everything looks incredible. Your attention to detail is fantastic.' They were kind words but fell flat and didn't contain his usual warm and complimentary tone. At their table was Blake's mother and Luke's friends who would be groomsmen tomorrow. These men would sit at the bridal table, but tonight, Luke and Juliette were flanked by her parents and bridesmaids.

'Is your dad coming?' Adele was aware their parents had divorced acrimoniously. Blakes's father had been unfaithful many times throughout his marriage to Phillipa. The family had splintered after the separation, the divisions clear, but Luke kept in touch.

'No. He's overseas. Has a new girlfriend and they are living in the States.'

'And he's not travelling back for the wedding?'

Blake shook his head. What did Blake think of their dad? With an unfaithful wife, the truth of his dad's actions must hit close to home. Both brothers adored their mother. She rested her hand on his thigh under the table but Blake turned away and spoke to the man on his left.

Background music played from a list prepared by her, and the main meal was served. Smelling delicious, Adele couldn't wait to try the lamb. Her mouth salivated as the plate was presented, but there was a commotion at the front table. Clare jumped up and raced towards the nearest row of vines, hunching over, sick.

Rushing over, Adele patted her back as she retched, the poor girl labouring to breathe. Hopefully puke helped cultivate the vines? After Clare had emptied the contents of her stomach, Adele handed her a disinfectant cloth. She smiled, vindicated in always having wipes on hand. Leaning on a rickety vine fence, Clare's face was ashen and Adele insisted she go to bed and rest. The things one had to do as a wedding planner!

'Ad!' Luke shouted upon her return. Everyone had finished their meal, hers sat untouched, the lamb fat congealing on her plate. She wanted to sit down and devour the meal, but instead, plastered a smile to her face.

'Grab your dinner and sit with us. If Clare is sick tomorrow, you'll have to sub in as bridesmaid.'

'What? Oh no, I'm sure she'll be fine after a good sleep tonight.'

Luke gestured again to the now spare seat. Adele collected her plate, accepting a glare from Blake, and sat next to Juliette who ignored her and spoke French to her friends seated on the other side. Adele nibbled at her cold dinner. Moments later, Luke disappeared inside on the proviso of getting another drink despite the table service.

Adele pushed aside the plate and excused herself on the preface of having jobs to perform. Wandering inside, Luke was at the bar with his friends, watching footy on the television. Her team was playing and Adele was desperate to watch it too, but needs must! The opposition scored a goal and the small crowd erupted in cheer. The man in front of her celebrated with a victory salute but misjudged his step and his pint of beer sloshed over Adele, the liquid soaking into her hair and trickling down the side of her face and neck. Closing her eyes and clenching her jaw against the sensation didn't help.

'Hey mate, watch it!' In a guise of helping, Luke glided his hands roughly across her head and down the front of her drenched dress, brushing his fingertips across her breasts. His arm came to rest on her hip, dangerously close to her bottom.

She'd dreamed of this sort of touch, well perhaps not exactly like this, but Luke's touch and attention and now, scrunched under his arm, his body smelling of stale beer, wet hair hanging in her eyes, it was all shades of wrong.

'Shouldn't you be outside spending time with your future wife and guests?' she spluttered, controlling her urge to flee, and struggling to ignore the sensation of disgust that spread throughout her body at the droplets of beer sliding towards her ankles.

Luke didn't remove his eyes from the television. 'I do, I should be, I want to. But I want to watch the footy too, you know? And Juliette doesn't understand Aussie rules.' He sipped his drink. 'You know what, Ad?' He faced her then. 'I'm so happy you're here. Being together is wonderful, being in love is wonderful. You're always here when I need you. In the good times and the bad. You're extraordinary. Our relationship is special. We have a real connection, soul mates, that's what we are. You understand me, care about me, we can talk, have fun...'

Adele's heart hammered so fast the whole room must have heard. These words, the ones she'd longed to hear...She snuggled in closer to his side, the sticky beer on her skin forgotten. 'I agree, Luke.' Her words came out too fast. 'We are special together, have been friends for such a long time. It's unique. We know each other better than anyone.'

Waiters passed with plates of dessert and Luke dropped his arm and flung it in front of the closest attendant to force him to stop. Caught by surprise, the waiter, holding six plates, three on each arm lost his balance and the plates crashed to the polished concrete floor of the bar.

Adele ducked her head against smashing China. Blake was by her side in an instant. How'd he get there so fast?

Luke laughed, collected a piece of broken plate and using his fingers scooped pavlova straight into his mouth.

BLAKE HADN'T MEANT TO EAVESDROP. HE'D GONE INSIDE TO check on dinner service and the footy score. He hadn't expected to see Adele and Luke hugged up and whispering to each other right in front of the television. Despite the noise in the bar, their every word was loud and clear, the sound of everything else muted.

It wasn't necessarily the spoken words though; it was the look on Adele's face. It was like a punch straight to his gut. Her face tilted upwards to his brother, eyes open wide, lips parted, vulnerable, completely devoted and smitten. Adoring. The look of a woman in love.

It made sense to him now. Her commitment to making this the best wedding ever, her over-the-top attention and worship of Luke.

Adele was in love with Luke.

Luke who was getting married to Juliette tomorrow. His guts churned. How could he have been so stupid?

Had it all been a ruse? Was it her plan to steal Luke away before the vows were exchanged? No...he couldn't believe it, didn't want to believe it. And surely her attempts to create a beautiful wedding failed to achieve that goal?

Until...his attention was diverted by crashing plates.

'Dave, are you okay, mate?' He stepped in as plates of food smashed to the ground, cream and crumbs and sliced fruit covering the surface. His bloody brother again, causing a mess. Blake ensured his staff member wasn't hurt and then helped clean up. Adele stood frozen for a moment before launching into action. Luke ate the ruined dessert. And drank beer.

Once the area was cleared of cake and shrapnel, Blake touched his brother on the arm. Luke flung back in surprise and then bellowed with laugher.

'You've had enough. It's the night before your wedding, mate. You can't be getting plastered and waking up with a hang-over.' This evoked more obnoxious throaty chuckles.

'Adele'll fix it. She'll have a remedy, a cure, that woman can fix anything! Well, for me anyways.' His words were too loud. 'There isn't anything she won't do for me...' Action on the TV caught his attention and he paused mid-sentence. Blake waited, his eyes skittering to Adele who stood to the side of them, dish cloth in one hand and a broken shard of plate in the other.

'Doesn't sound like much of a friendship to me.'

'Aw, you're jealous! Two women love me, and you've got none. You're alone in your fancy vineyard,' he emphasised the word vineyard as if it was dirty, 'but Adele loves me.'

Blake wished Adele would move away, not hear any more of Luke's drunk talk. But she stood still like a statute taking in each word his brother spewed out.

'Don't you mean Juliette?'

'Yes, yes, I do! She's going to be my wife. She loves me.' It wasn't lost on Blake that Luke wasn't declaring his love for anyone. As an afterthought, his brother added with a smirk, 'but Adele does, too!'

In that moment, Blake loathed his brother. Reminded him

of his father; the father they rarely saw now because he had moved onto his next girlfriend, a string of many, after his mother threw him out. That caused an ache to his chest, an ache for his mother left behind. Of course, Blake knew that feeling, too. Blake was a straight up bloke, but there were a few things he didn't tolerate and infidelity and dishonesty were two of them.

Were his brother and Adele guilty?

Perhaps Luke carried their father's genes? Addicted to the chase and the thrill of being adored, not by one woman, but many. It was confusing because Blake got the sense Luke didn't truly want Adele - only the endless devotion she showed him. To bolster his ego, no doubt. But what did he know? Perhaps Luke was also secretly in love with Adele?

He hung his head. Adele, headfast and strong and determined. Why didn't she step in and say something? Halt the diarrhoea spewing from Luke's mouth, defend herself...Deny the accusations, claw back some self-worth? Blake wouldn't let it continue.

'Okay, that's enough. Let's get you to bed.' Luke shook off Blake's hand and more beer splattered the floor as he toppled. The crowd erupted in further chants at the score on the television.

Adele dumped the items in her hands and rushed forwards and grasped Luke's other arm. Together they hauled him to his feet. Luke flashed a grin at Blake that said: *I told you so.* Adele whispered into his ear and Luke nodded.

'I'll go to bed because Adele said so and she'll take me. You'll tuck me in, won't you Adele?' he crooned. Avoiding his eye, the pair left the bar.

Blake didn't understand his growing feelings for Adele, but

nonetheless he stood feeling desolate. And he wasn't even sure why. It was easy to avoid relationships, perhaps he'd been hoping for more; hoping that Adele was genuine and sincere and, well, different. His ex-wife had taught him a valuable lesson – not to trust and she'd been right, he didn't. And that had stood him in good stead, so far. His barriers remained in force, hard and strong. Had been since she'd left him. He understood where devotion and unconditional love got you, kicked to the kerb and left behind.

If he'd been beginning to trust her, now he didn't. It was that simple.

Anger surged through him at his brother for using Adele, and then for her allowing it. How could she be so stupid? Or was he disappointed? Yeah, disappointed but also vindicated. Women couldn't be trusted and Adele had proven that tonight.

With a twisted gut, he hoped that the two of them were not together, in bed, right now.

He didn't know whether that wish was for him, Adele, or Luke and Juliette. What a mess.

# 8
---

*Saturday: the day of the wedding*

Running along the uneven stone path, Adele blinked through the heavy raindrops lashing her face. Thunder clapped causing her to jump, and suddenly the track was illuminated by a streak of lightning filling the darkened sky.

The ground was soggy and she slipped as she hurried. The wind whistled through the tops of the trees and the sound whipped in her ears.

A quick glance at her smartwatch told her it was nearing five-thirty am.

Reaching the outdoor area where they'd eaten last night, the tables and chairs were toppled, and in between the sky being lit up, she could make out the leaves and fallen branches strewn everywhere. After her dire embarrassment last night at the scene with Luke, she hadn't cleared the tables. Now everything was a tangled mess on the ground beaten by the relentless rain. Ignoring the sharp pricks to her skin, Adele scrambled to collect as much as she could in one handful and raced under cover of the verandah. The relief from the rain was instant but there was loads more stuff to save. Taking a deep breath, she ran back out. A hand touched her shoulder and Blake shouted in her ear. 'Help me with the tables.' She nodded and together they carried the long timber tables followed by the chairs.

Wiping moisture from her eyes, she readied herself for the next trip. Blake gripped her arm, his eyes flicking to her chest where her wet pjs clung to her breasts. She puffed out her shirt only for it to return to exactly the same spot.

'Leave the rest. We've got the tables and chairs, that's the most important because we'll need them later. The rest might be ruined,' he paused at her sob, 'but they aren't essential for the wedding. It's too dangerous in this weather.'

Tears streamed down Adele's cheeks, but Blake didn't comfort her. The Blake she'd met only a few short days ago would have offered support and reassurances while holding her close. Things had changed between them after last night.

She glanced away from him to the scene of destruction in front of her. All her hard work, wasted. But he was right. None of it was needed today. Everything could be thrown out when the storm passed, and oh, how she wished that would be mercifully quick.

'I need to check the alpacas. You head back to bed. We'll sort this out later in the morning.' He paused. 'It'll be alright.' But didn't people always say that even when they could never be sure of the outcome? Nonetheless, she nodded.

Watching Blake race away into the darkness, Adele spotted the bike. Oh no! A quick glance at the sky and she hurried back out into the elements to wheel it across the grass. Half-way along the soaked ground and she slipped and landed on her backside, the spiky pedal digging into her arm. 'Damnit!' There was a little nudge to her arm accompanied by a whine and Marshmallow was at her side. 'Oh, sweetie.' The dog was drenched, its curly fur crimped and bedraggled. 'Let's get inside, quick!'

She parked the bike haphazardly amongst the other items on the deck and encouraged the dog indoors. 'Let's get you warm.'

Hurrying inside to Blake's rooms, she found a towel and dried off the dog. It was a rather successful way of avoiding touching it directly. Why hadn't she thought of it before? His other dogs, obviously frightened of the storm, huddled in his living area. Slumping into a nearby chair, she used the protection of the towel to pet each of them in turn, and spoke reassuringly, and located a few dog treats before washing her hands.

What was she going to do? Storms passed quickly, right? So this one should be no different. Hard to imagine as the rain pelted against the window frames and thunder rocked the sky. A bright day would dawn with blue skies and warm sun and this would be nothing but a bad nightmare...Tucked into the towel, she cuddled Marshmallow to her chest and the dog snuggled there comfortably. It was exactly the comfort she needed.

The wedding was the least of her worries, she'd pull it off, no question. Regardless of circumstances, that is what she did and did well. But how she'd behaved last night; she cringed at the memory. Luke had been downright offensive, basically calling her a servant, or slave or a what? What did you call a person who acquiesced to another's commands without independent thought? Oh, she didn't know, her mind was addled. But worse, when did she become that person? She was strong, independent, intelligent and yet what he said was true. She'd become nothing, a shadow waiting in the wings for the man she wanted to love her to drip feed her a minute of his time. And he bloody well knew it and feasted upon her adoration most unkindly.

She had been a right royal idiot.

And the look on Blake's face. He'd seen right through her. He knew, and his face not only expressed his disbelief, also his disappointment. But disappointment at what exactly? Her acting as a pathetic needy woman, or something else...Her eyes blinked a few times and she fell asleep.

BLAKE RUBBED HIS TEMPLES AND FOUND, FOR ONCE, HE DIDN'T have a headache. Weird, he had them more than he didn't, so when his mind was clear, it was a strange sensation, particularly after only a few short hours of sleep. The rain had eased but it still fell from a cloudy and grey sky. Nearing eight o'clock now, he'd come back for some grub and a coffee before pushing on and making the end of this day much better than the start.

Inside was quiet. Rarely did he lock up the dogs, but in this weather, he'd had no choice. But he expected them to be going crazy in the small confines of his rooms. He listened again. Nope, nothing.

Walking into the living room, he heard a soft purr, more like a cat than a dog. Sleeping animals were spread across the rug and around the furniture. In the armchair, Adele was curled up, fast asleep, Marshmallow cocooned in her lap. His heart skipped a beat and he wished it didn't. Angelic in sleep, her still moist hair clung in strands around her face, her lips were parted and her long lashes fluttered.

The dogs sensed his presence, one woke and then the remainder. Marshmallow jumped from Adele's lap and licked at his ankles. Adele woke, raised her head and stretched it left and right. 'Oh, what's the time?'

Blake moved closer, his fingers connecting with a few wisps of her tousled hair, but he pulled back, balled his hand into a fist and held it by his side. 'Not long gone eight.' Hands on the armrests to pull herself up, he stopped her with raised palms. 'Listen for a moment. It's taken time but Cam and I have cleaned the back shed for the reception. We had to gurney away the dirt and have now left it to air, but it's spotless and a perfect place for the reception. Not sure what you were thinking, but I've also cleared the verandah and we can open the restaurant doors and that might make a nice space for the ceremony.'

Adele watched him and he saw her mind tick over. Before she could ask, he continued. 'Nope, the grass is soaked and it's still raining. Even if it dried up right this minute, the ground is cactus. It would be impossible for women dressed in their lovely clothes and high heel shoes to walk across the grass, let alone a bride with a full-length gown.'

'You've done all that? You haven't been back to bed?'

'Yes and no. We've hauled all the tables and chairs into the shed, but it's otherwise bare waiting for your final touch. Oh, and the other thing, because it's so muddy, we've laid hay across the grass. Later, the red carpet can go on top of the hay to avoid it sinking. And we thought you might like a couple of bales to spread around the barn or outside, for decoration or something. Up to you.' He shrugged and his words petered away.

'That's incredible. I can work with that. Thank you. As long as the bride approves.'

'She doesn't have much choice.'

Adele nodded. 'I'd better get straight on to it, lots to do.'

The air between them remained electric, but everything was different. Gone was the joking, the banter, and fun. Gone were those killer smiles she offered in his direction. Now it was stilted and uncomfortable, as if they were strangers.

Nothing to do but let her go.

'ADELE!'

Before responding to the panicked call, she positioned the last bonbonniere on the table and admired her work. Perfect.

'Adele! Clare's still vomiting and has a fever and can't get out of bed. Juliette needs you to fill in as bridesmaid.' Olivia begged. 'Please.' She softened her tone.

Adele sighed. Hadn't she done enough already? 'You know what, Olivia, I'll do pretty much anything to make this wedding amazing, but truly? Juliette doesn't want me in her bridal party. Won't it ruin her day?'

Olivia shook her head fast and furious. 'No. She's a realist. There are three best men. If there aren't matching bridesmaids, the whole symmetry is off. The photos will look ridiculous, and you need to make a speech! Both Bethany and I are terrified of public speaking, we can't do it!'

Working tirelessly all day, Adele remained shamelessly in her pjs, hadn't dressed or eaten. The ceremony space was ready and she was finalising the shed. She let Olivia's words sink in, looked around, chuffed at what she'd created. Juliette may not be happy they weren't sitting under the glorious Australian stars, but this room was magic. In fact, the country iron shed added to the effect with its rusted red and stained walls and concrete floor. The haybales were a fantastic addition to the Australiana of the theme and the white blooms and greenery another contrasting pop of colour. Foliage hung delicately from the ceiling mixed in with white, bright fairy lights. Elegant and divine, simple, and beautiful: as the bride ordered.

While the scene might be spectacular, Adele knew when she was beaten. She'd accepted hours ago that she simply needed to make this wedding great and then she'd be getting the hell of out here, away from Bellethorpe and the disaster this entire week had become. And away from Luke who in only a few short hours would become her married best friend.

The wedding would be a success but otherwise, she'd failed. Luke had not made declarations of love. In fact, he'd been very clear about the nature of their one-sided friendship. The word 'toad' came to mind. But it wasn't his fault, she'd lost her way. Strangely, she felt more wretched about the realisation of what she'd become and how pathetic she must appear to Blake, than of her lost chance with Luke. Blake had certainly backed off since. Geez, she was mortified at her own behaviour.

So, what was one more to add to the endless list of things she did for Luke? This request was a tough one, though, it was personal, and she thought of Blake, again. He was all she could think about these last few hours. Would he think her weak for giving in and acquiescing again? Always doing Luke's bidding? Or would he appreciate that she'd helped the family in a time of need? She didn't know.

'Okay. I'm done here anyway, let's go.'

~

THIS WAS THE MOMENT OF HER DREAMS. HER WALKING DOWN THE aisle towards her beloved, Luke who stood at the altar. Looking drop-dead gorgeous in his tuxedo and black tie with tails, clean-shaven and boyish, with his hair freshly cut and wearing a smile filled with emotion, just for her. In the background classical music played by a string quartet. The moment was perfect and shivers raced up her spine.

Except, it wasn't for her.

After a skimmed glance in her direction, Luke focused on the bride that followed. Adele's eyes scanned the crowd searching for one person. Despite the predicament she found herself in, her spirits lifted immediately. He was still, had always been, the sunshine in her day over this past week.

Now, he stood in the blessed sun, against the nearby fence, away from the guests spanning the verandah of his homestead. Adele walked on wobbly feet hungry to devour him. Rewarded, their eyes connected and for a few precious moments they were the only two people present. Well, that's how it played out in her mind. Blake was far enough away that she couldn't quite catch the nuances of his face or read his thoughts.

In a show of community spirit that Bellethorpe was well-known for, Caleb and Bridie stood with their daughter, Sybella, and Cam, Lily the florist and Sheila and Peter from the antique store. Next to them was Simone, cake maker extraordinaire and a few other locals she recognised. There was Jacqueline Kennedy, the mayor and lifeblood of the town. They hadn't met, but she'd been pointed out to Adele on many occasions; her reputation preceded her.

Blake stood amongst them with one foot resting on the

lowest paling of the fence. In front of him the dogs sat to attention, wearing pink bows. At the sight of Marshmallow, her heart melted. Behind the locals, the alpacas spanned the perimeter of the fence wearing matching, larger pink bows around their long necks. None of the animals moved and the scene was more perfect than the wedding she'd created. Okay, maybe not perfect; pink wouldn't have been her choice of colour for the bows, it didn't exactly fit with the theme, but hey, what woman didn't love pink, especially when worn by an animal?

Tears welled and fear gripped her belly like a vice. Had she made a great mistake? Arriving at the head of the carpet, she forced her gaze away from Blake and moved into position before the celebrant, waiting for the bride. Every guest focused on the red carpet; except her: she gazed at Luke and his glistening tears, emotion evident on his face, wonderment at the beauty walking towards him. Luke loved Juliette. And for the first time, she was happy for her friend.

Her friend. It would take a while but she'd adjust. To her astonishment, her heart didn't shatter into a million pieces, nor did her life end. Her desire was to see Blake; it took willpower to remain focused until Luke kissed his bride, the crowd cheered and at last, she glanced over her shoulder, but Blake was gone.

What a fool she'd been.

Blake's defences melted away until he was a vulnerable, messy heap, dizzy with desire at Adele in that dress. Tight, fitting snugly around her curves, the low neckline emphasised her cleavage. The pale apricot didn't match the pink strands of her hair that had been dulled for the occasion and sat amongst long, blonde waves, but illuminated her skin so that it glowed in the bright afternoon rays of light.

He might be feeling exposed and unsteady on his feet, but he refused to acknowledge the glances Adele had thrown his way during the ceremony. No point. And he wasn't sure what they meant anyway. Was she more like Luke than he'd realised? Hedging her bets both ways? And now that the wedding was in motion, she had to consider other options?

Didn't matter how stunning she was, she loved his brother, and he'd never take second place. He had other things to focus on anyway. Drowning some pain relief with a glass of water, he followed it swiftly with more beer. Then another. Adele was about to give her speech.

*JULIETTE AND LUKE, ON BEHALF OF THE BRIDESMAIDS MY DUTY IS TO speak about the bride. Unfortunately, I don't know you well yet, Juliette. But in the last few hours I've gathered snippets that your family and friends have shared with me...Adele shared half a dozen stories others had generously provided to her. But more importantly they told me about the love you have found with Luke. And that Luke returns for you. It's true it has been a whirlwind relationship but there's no denying the love and affection you hold for each other. And everyone here wishes you all the very best for a wonderful and bright future together.*

*I do know Luke as we've been friends since we were sixteen and he offered to escort me to my semi-formal. He was a friend of a friend and lent a girl without a date a lifeline. Since then, we've been close mates and he's offered me many lifelines, probably too many and I've relied upon him too much. Luke has taught me about love and there have been many times I wished we could be more than friends. But seeing Luke with you Juliette, his beautiful bride this week and meeting your family, I realised I was wrong about the nature of our love. Yes, I love you, Luke, like a brother where we care deeply about one another, and fight as only siblings can, but we do not share the love you have with Juliette.*

ADELE TURNED AWAY FROM LUKE AND SEARCHED THE CROWD until she found him. An army of heads swung in his direction and Blake lowered his head, the beer he'd drunk burning his chest.

*OVER THIS PAST CRAZY WEEK, I'VE LEARNED A LOT ABOUT LOVE. LOVE is sharing intimacy with someone special. It's about sharing small, what might seem insignificant things and little moments. Things like being rescued out of a muddy puddle after being attacked by an alpaca; wiping away alpaca saliva even though it's disgusting; making breakfast and coffee without expecting it in return; sharing home-cooked food; singing in the shower and not caring that they hear; caring for others and animals; teaching one another, for example, about fine wine; helping each other without being asked; sharing your inner-most thoughts and fears without reprisal and only offering support; loving not only their body, but their soul and understanding them and what they are passionate about; listening when they are frightened and unsure; caring about their feelings and responses and actions; desiring to be with them all of the time; thinking about them all of the time; and most of all understanding when you are wrong and seeking forgiveness.*

. . .

HIS HEAD THROBBED, EACH THUD LIKE AN EXPLODING firecracker. He needed air and stood and left the shed. Was she saying what he thought? Was she expressing...feelings for him? The room that had been rambunctiously loud, was suddenly quiet as he made his exit. Adele faltered for the briefest moment and then continued her speech. Outside he leaned back against the wall and listened in privacy without the surreptitious glances of the crowd.

*I SEE MANY OF THESE ATTRIBUTES BETWEEN THE TWO OF YOU, Juliette and Luke and I envy that and hope that you shall be very happy together.*

THERE WAS THE TINKLE OF GLASS AGAINST GLASS AND THE CHEERS of toast. A gush of air followed the opening of the shed doors. He didn't turn.

'HAVE I COMPLETELY SCREWED THINGS UP? ARE YOU SO ANGRY you can't forgive me?'

It was excruciating waiting for his reply. Blake stared, hard, intently into her soul, ripping open her wounds and leaving her exposed.

'Do you love Luke?'

Now she hung her head, her hair covering her face. 'I thought I did. I thought I loved him for a long time. But I was a silly girl infatuated with a boy that didn't return my affections.

And I hung around like a love-sick puppy waiting, thinking I was good enough and eventually he'd notice me.'

'And hold the best wedding ever for him in the hope that at the very last minute, he'd pause the ceremony and declare his love for you?'

'Well, when you say it like that, it sounds stupid.' They both laughed, releasing a little tension.

'I was wrong, Blake. Very wrong. I realise that now.'

'You were wrong about a few things. One of those is that you are enough Adele. But...' she swallowed at his pause. 'My wife left me for my best mate, she betrayed me. I can't be, won't be second best...I need to be able to trust that you want me, only me. That you won't change your mind, leave me for a better option. My next relationship must work. I can't fail again.'

'I would never...'

'But forget all that Adele. You know I have a diagnosed brain injury from the concussions that caused my retirement. It's manageable now, but it might deteriorate. Worst case scenario it could turn into dementia, or long-term chronic migraines. It's not fair to make anyone else suffer or be part of my suffering. This life I've created for myself, out here, it works now. I'm happy...'

'I understand your wife hurt you, she did a terrible thing, knocking you when you were already down, betraying you and your trust. But you know me already, I'm not like that. I mean, let's be honest, I've waited twelve years for one man to notice me...'

'Yet up until today, you loved him, until he wasn't yours anymore...'

'I've explained that, if you can't accept my excuse,' she

shrugged, 'there's nothing else I can say, other than I was clearly always looking at the wrong brother. You are nothing like him.' She laughed. 'You are kind and funny and serious and careful and empathetic...' To help her cause Marshmallow appeared out of nowhere and rubbed her little body against their legs. Blake picked her up and Adele continued. 'Who else saves stranded animals and loves their alpacas so wholeheartedly? Blake, you have so much to give, so much love and attention and time. You should not be alone. And as for your injury, well, that is who you are. I can help you, on the Estate, be company on lonely evenings, administer paracetamol...I'll make you even happier. Together.'

'Wait what, you'd move here?'

'Yes. I would make the best wedding co-ordinator the Kingsley Estate has ever seen!'

'That's a bit rich. Then we'd have to go through this palaver each weekend.'

'Yes, something you're very good at, I might add. That show with the dogs and alpacas. Sweet.'

Blake reached for her hand. He cuddled the dog with the other, holding it close. 'Did anything ever happen with my brother?' His voice waivered.

'Never.' Pause. 'I would not lie to you.'

'I believe you.' He moved closer so their bodies touched. 'I've been dying to do this since that first night.' When he moved within inches of her mouth, his warm breath kissed her skin, and her knees trembled. Blake placed Marshmallow on the ground where she gazed adoringly at them both. The cool breeze caused ripples to erupt along her skin, the sensation cascading through her body. Finally, his warm, moist lips met hers, their bodies crushing together with need, heat radiating between them, her body thrumming. Releasing each other to catch their breath, her lips burned for more, for him, for the kiss never to end.

'Oh, there's only one thing,' she pulled back creating space between them. 'You'll have to start barracking for Hawthorn. It's a deal breaker.'

Blake laughed so that his body shook before showering her with another kiss: long, sweet and smouldering. 'Agreed.'

# EPILOGUE

*One year later*

'Oh my gosh! This is the best one yet!'

'You say that about every wedding!' Blake's laugh resonated deep from his belly while he took in his surrounds. Adele stood a few feet from the bride and groom who were seated to sign the formal marriage certificate. She glowed with happiness, her face adorning a smile from cheek to cheek. Today she was kitted out in brown and orange, with matching tangerine shaded strands of hair for the occasion. Not her usual colour choice and it wasn't for the wedding. Hawthorn had made it to a preliminary final that was airing later in the day, during the reception. They'd already agreed to keep one another updated on the score.

But Blake agreed. This wedding was pretty spectacular. Kingsley Estate had become in high demand as a wedding venue and it had hosted an array of varied weddings, from the elegant and traditional to the interesting and far out. His mind boggled at the range of themes people engaged for their special today.

Blake had always known that Adele was good at her job, he'd witnessed it firsthand after all, but watching her in motion this last year, he almost burst with pride. Planning wasn't her only forte, she'd become their expert marketer and not only had the wedding business exploded, the Estate with its winery had benefited also. And of course, with weddings, came accommodation and the cabins were rarely empty.

Adele Bastian-Jones had breathed new life not only into him, but to the Estate. And he still glowed warm in her presence. Who'd have thought that one woman could break down his barriers and teach him to love again. The relationship they'd created was of them against the world, of safety and security and with Adele by his side, he could conquer anything. Or at least the ability to tackle whatever they may face, together.

Never one to shy away from things, Adele had suggested a simple spiral-bound notebook as a way for him to keep track of things he'd usually forget. He was hesitant, after all his mind should be good enough, but it had worked. He fingered the pocket of his trousers and felt the sharp corner of the book. Nearby, was a medical emergency kit with every conceivable drug he might need. Again, with Adele's help he had worked out ways to lessen the severity of the headaches by treating them quickly. Small and simple steps. None of it changed his condition, but immeasurably improved his day to day. It took practice but now he didn't suffer any embarrassment about pulling out his notebook to check a fact or someone's name.

There would be no forgetting today though. This couple

married in amongst special guests: the attacking alpacas. It had remained an ongoing joke.

Even Adele had learned things in the last twelve months. Glancing at her now, bolts of pleasure and excitement shot through him. With low levels of exposure, Adele was better managing her compulsion to germs. It wasn't fixed, most likely never would be, but it had improved. Today she held Cookie's leash, one of their eldest and most placid alpacas. Occasionally, it reared back and its fur brushed against her cheek but she didn't flinch. One of the wedding guests fed Cookie with grains, the animal's saliva dripping from her mouth and Adele didn't grimace. She kept a watchful eye on the guest to ensure everyone's safety. Being spat on would never be her favourite thing and that was fair enough.

Her constant companion Marshmallow had grown into a young dog and raced around her legs. The dog matched its owner with a band of brown and orange attached to its collar.

With a pause in the proceedings to allow guests to congratulate the couple, Adele wandered closer to where he stood with a bunch of other alpacas, waiting for their part in the event.

'Did you ever think you'd be combining your love of alpacas and weddings?' Her smile was beguiling and bewitched him each and every time.

'I do not have a love of weddings, unless perhaps it's our own.'

Adele's beaming smile dropped. It wasn't often she was uncertain, but now was one of those times.

He turned her away from the crowd and with an alpaca on each side and a menagerie of dogs running around his feet, he kneeled. 'Adele, these last twelve months have been amazing, the best of my life. You've adapted not only to country life but to living at the Estate and have developed a thriving business, along with a love of wine and dirty animals. Who would have imagined you'd wash your hands less often? When I thought I was lost and alone, you arrived here and messed up my miserable existence. You showed me how much life there is to live and how to love again. And helped me move on from a painful chapter in my life. I love you and want you by my side, always. Will you marry me?'

Adele mopped at the tears streaming down her cheeks with the scarf she wore and nodded. Blake ruffled around in the fur of the closest alpaca and extracted a case. He rose and extended the box, flipping open the lid to reveal an antique diamond engagement ring. He slipped it on her finger.

'Blake, I am so thankful for that day I rocked up here and fell into the mud and you rescued me. Not only from the attacking alpaca but from the life I was living. You saved me, too, when I didn't even know I needed saving. From a life of being in the shadows, unnoticed and unappreciated to being in the spotlight. Every day with you is special and you make me feel loved and adored and so happy, I love you and cannot wait to marry you.'

He claimed her lips in a deep, sensual kiss. The embrace was passionate, scintillating and sent spirals of desire straight to his core. When they broke apart, Adele was unsteady on her feet and bounced on her toes.

'Can I coordinate our wedding?'

'Duh, of course.'

'And we can get married here at the Estate?'

'Yes, nowhere else would be right.'

'And we can serve your award-winning Verdelho? I'm still so excited you won!'

'That goes without saying!'

'And we can have alpacas and dogs and...'

'Whatever you want.' And Blake swooped in for another peck, but she ducked with a titter and his lips landed on her earlobe. He teased her there instead, and she moaned before leaning away.

'Maybe a Hawthorn themed wedding this time next year when the Hawks play in the grand final!?'

'Except that...' He showered her face with feather light kisses.

'Yeah, agreed, no football celebration, we need to watch the game. But what about a Christmas wedding? With the help of the Christmas tree farm nearby...'

Blake kissed her again without reply.

'Gosh, my name is going to be a mouthful isn't it? Adele Bastian-Jones-Kingsley.'

Blake tore his lips away from her smooth and pink cheek to check if she was joking. She remained poker-faced. 'If that's what you want, honey.'

# ABOUT THE AUTHOR

Leanne Lovegrove is a lawyer, wife and mother and a lover of romance and reading. Her law career created an addiction to coffee but provides countless story ideas. She is the author of five romance novels, and this is her fourth novella and second novella in her small town Bellethorpe series. Leanne writes sweeping love stories with happily-ever-afters with strong female heroines and set in the beautiful landscape of Australia. She lives in Brisbane, Australia with her husband and three children.

To find out more about Leanne's books, you can find her here:
www.leannelovegroveauthor.com

Bookbub:
https://www.bookbub.com/profile/leanne-lovegrove

## ALSO BY LEANNE LOVEGROVE

Love the small town of Bellethorpe? Catch up on the first in the series
- *Love in Between*

*Caleb Stirling has never had it easy, but he's worked hard and is a stellar chef of his own five-star restaurant in Sydney. Over one fateful week his world crumbles around him and he finds himself in an outback country town where everything he's ever known is threatened.*

*Bridie Finch is the lifeblood of Bellethorpe. Need something done? Give it to Bridie. She's so busy looking after the community, her father and their strawberry farm, she fails to care for herself.*

*Now, Caleb must care for his orphaned niece. But Bridie needs a chef for the annual Bastille Day Festival and, unwillingly, he lands the role. But there's no place to hide in town and soon the locals discover who he really is. Instead of rejecting him, they rally with support and quickly both Bellethorpe and Bridie get under his skin.*

*Unexpectedly, city slicker Caleb finds himself a single dad and part of a thriving community, and undeniably attracted to wholesome country girl, Bridie. Whilst she's happy to offer support, can she deal with his inner demons, and will Bridie let him help her, too?*

*A sweet small-town story of community, being accepted and finding love in the most unexpected of places.*

**Here's what reviewers are saying about Love in Between:**

*A scrumptious read, devoured this one in one sitting* – Leonie, Goodreads

*This beautifully written emotional story will have you cheering for Bridie, who quietly gives her all to the town and the new city guy. Caleb is out of his comfort zone in more ways than one, but he tries. This stand-out, brave romantic story is well worth it. Couldn't wait to see how it all turned out. Recommend* – Louise, Goodreads

*This is a moving and beautiful story that is sure to make any true romance readers heart soar with happiness* – Helen, Goodreads

# LEANNE'S OTHER NOVELS:

*Novels:*

Unexpected Delivery

Illegal Love

Keeper of the Light

A Good Life

Her Outback Home

*Novellas:*

Escapades of a Personal Stylist

Love on the Sweeping Plains

Love in Between (Bellethorpe #1)

*Anthologies*

Love in a Sunburnt Land vol 1

Love in a Sunburnt Land vol 2

www.ingramcontent.com/pod-product-compliance
Lightning Source LLC
Chambersburg PA
CBHW030414120726
47904CB00007B/2273